LOVE ON THE UPBEAT

April glanced over at Todd and found him watching her. "I thought we were here to admire the scenery," she teased.

"I am." He moved closer, looking down at her.

April felt the warmth spread up her face. *There I go again! Why can't I just be cool?* she asked herself.

Todd touched her cheek. "You're cute when you blush," he said softly.

Suddenly April knew he was going to kiss her. What should she do? Though she longed for his kiss, she was afraid that her response would reveal how little experience she'd had kissing boys.

As he lowered his face to hers someone called out from just below the place where they were standing, "Hey! Anyone up there?"

"Perfect timing," Todd grumbled.

Bantam Sweet Dreams romances
Ask your bookseller for the books you have missed

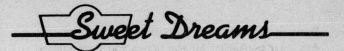

LOVE ON
THE UPBEAT

June O'Connell

BANTAM BOOKS

NEW YORK • TORONTO • LONDON • SYDNEY • AUCKLAND

RL 6, age 11 and up

LOVE ON THE UPBEAT
A Bantam Book / July 1992

ISBN 0-553-29455-5

Published simultaneously in the United States and Canada

*Bantam Books are published by Bantam Books, a division
of Bantam Doubleday Dell Publishing Group, Inc. Its trademark, consisting of the words "Bantam Books" and the
portrayal of a rooster, is Registered in U.S. Patent and
Trademark Office and in other countries. Marca Regis-
trada. Bantam Books, 666 Fifth Avenue, New York, New
York 10103.*

PRINTED IN THE UNITED STATES OF AMERICA

OPM   0 9 8 7 6 5 4 3 2 1

To my daughter, Kelly, who shared her experiences at Arrowbar Music Camp and to Ron and B.J. who livened up the vocal sessions

Chapter One

"I wonder if I really sing well enough to be going to music camp," April Sullivan murmured, more to herself than to her mother. "I'll probably be the worst one there."

She leaned back against the seat of the car as her mother concentrated on the mountain curves. The sheer drop off one side of the road made April shudder as she looked down. She turned away from the window and slumped deeper into her seat. Not even the scary hairpin turns could take her mind off her worries.

Mrs. Sullivan gave her a quick look. "April, don't be silly. You have a lovely voice."

"Yeah—to *you*, Mom."

"You've never had doubts about your singing before," her mother said. "You'll be fine, and you'll make lots of new friends."

April rolled her eyes. *What I really need,* she thought, *is to have Mom turn the car around and go back home.* "I sure wish Janie was coming," she said, already missing her best friend.

All spring and early summer they had planned for this month at Bear Mountain Music Camp. Janie had been to the vocal session last year, and she'd told April all about the singing and good times. They'd examined the camp brochure again and again, dreaming about the cute boys they'd meet and the fun they'd have. Now, without Janie, it just wouldn't be the same.

"It's too bad Janie's plans changed," Mrs. Sullivan agreed. "But who could turn down a trip to Europe?"

April closed her eyes. "I don't really blame her. But I'm so nervous that I'm getting butterflies in my stomach."

"Janie would certainly have made it easier at first." Her mother smiled encouragingly at April. "You'll fit right in as soon as you get acquainted with the other kids. Just give it time."

The pep talk again, April thought. *I don't think I can bear to hear it one more time!*

Mrs. Sullivan slowed the car next to a sign with an arrow pointing to a dirt road. "We're almost there. Help me look now."

April watched the trees and bushes by the side of the road as the car slowly climbed the sharp incline that led to a strange place, new people, and no special friend. Then she remembered the gorgeous guys Janie had showed her in last year's camp picture, and wondered if any of them would be back this summer. April smiled a little. Maybe her mother was right. Maybe camp wouldn't be so bad after all. And she *did* love to sing. . . .

A few minutes later, they entered the campground where a big sign welcomed them to Bear Mountain Music Camp.

"Do you want to unload your things now or find out about registration first?" Mrs. Sullivan asked.

"Let's get my stuff later." April glanced in the rearview mirror and brushed back her long, sandy blond hair, which was still wavy from her efforts with the curling iron earlier that morning, then frowned at the freckles that sprinkled the bridge of her nose.

"Coming?" her mother asked as she got out of the car. "They *do* have mirrors at camp, you know."

"Oh, Mom!" April slid out of the passenger side and tucked her blue T-shirt into the waistband of her shorts.

She noticed a group of teenagers laughing and talking under the roof of an open shelter some distance away. A few of the girls were paired up with boys, holding hands, while others sat together and chatted comfortably.

Everyone knows each other, April thought

3

dismally. *They're already friends, and here I am, alone. This is going to be even worse than I thought! If only Janie were here.* She watched as a girl arrived and was greeted with squeals of delight. "I wonder if anyone else but me is here for the first time," she whispered to her mother.

"There will be many new people," Mrs. Sullivan assured her. "And you'll meet them all very soon."

April wondered how her mom would have acted if this were *her* first day at camp. She'd probably have talked to everybody right away. *I've got to try,* April thought. She saw an attractive girl with a long, dark braid coming toward her, and forced herself to smile. "Hi!" she said loudly.

The girl glanced at April, then hurried past her without a word.

Terrific, April thought, disappointed. *This is going to be just awful.*

"Look at this, honey," Mrs. Sullivan said, pointing to a poster tacked up on a bulletin board outside the main building. "It's a list of the campers' hometowns. There are two other kids here from Spring Valley!"

April refused to look. "I probably don't know them."

Hearing running footsteps on the path behind her, she turned and stared as the best-looking boy she had ever seen jogged by. He had thick, sandy-colored hair, and was wear-

4

ing a red cutoff T-shirt. For a moment April seemed to forget her apprehension as she wondered who he was, and if he had a girlfriend.

After April had registered, she and her mother started back to the car to unload her gear. A tall, dark-haired girl left a group of campers and walked briskly toward them.

"Hi! I'm Jackie," she said cheerfully. "You're new, aren't you?"

April nodded. "This is my first time here. My name's April and this is my mom."

"Nice to meet you both. You're going to *love* Bear Mountain," Jackie said with a broad grin. "I'm a counselor this season, but I've been a camper here for years. Have you found your cabin yet?"

"No," April said. "I just finished registration, but I'm in Cabin One."

"Oh great! I'm in charge of that cabin. You'll find it right at the end of this path, down a few steps. I'll see you later!" She waved and moved on to speak to some other girls.

"She seems very nice. And friendly, too," Mrs. Sullivan said as they continued toward the car.

"Mom, she's a counselor. It's her *job* to be friendly," April pointed out grumpily. She hadn't seen another friendly face yet, or anyone she wanted to be friends with. Of course, there was that good-looking boy, but he hadn't paid any attention to her.

When they got to the car, April and her mother hauled out April's sleeping bag, her suitcase, a garment bag containing the dresses she would need for the concerts the campers gave, and her guitar case. April surveyed the pile in dismay. "I can't *believe* I'll need all this stuff!"

"You'll never be able to carry everything by yourself," Mrs. Sullivan worried. "Why don't you let me take some of your bags to the cabin and help you get settled in?"

April shook her head. "No thanks, Mom. I can manage on my own." She didn't want her bunkmates to think she was such a baby that her mother had to do things for her.

"Well, if you're sure, I guess I might as well be heading home," Mrs. Sullivan said. She gave April a big hug. "Have a wonderful time, honey! And don't forget to write—better yet, phone us when you have a minute. Dad, your brothers, and I want to hear all about how you're doing."

"I won't forget, Mom," April said, trying to sound a lot more cheerful than she felt.

As she watched her mother drive away, April felt terribly lonely. She missed her family already—well, maybe not her little brothers. Her mother was so sure that everything would work out well. April could only hope that she was right.

Now to find Cabin One. Staggering under the weight of her luggage, April left the parking lot and looked around for the path Jackie had pointed out. A group of girls, all wearing red T-shirts with "Riverside Madrigal Singers" printed on them, was passing by, and she asked for directions. One of the girls pointed toward a flight of wooden steps while the others looked at April without much interest. Feeling even more like an outsider, she started down the steps, and soon found Cabin One.

Hesitating by the open door, she heard voices inside, and tried to summon up the courage to face more strangers. Just as she thought she couldn't possibly do it, April heard a voice calling her name.

She turned and to her astonishment saw Karen Sanchez running down the steps behind her. She and Karen shared some classes at Spring Valley High, but they had never been close. Now, however, Karen looked like a long-lost friend.

"I missed you at registration," she cried. "When I saw your name on the list, I couldn't believe it!"

The girls stood grinning at each other while Karen caught her breath. "I didn't know you sang," she said at last. "You don't take choir at school."

"I wanted to, but I couldn't squeeze it into my schedule," April said.

7

"Well, how'd you know about music camp?"

"My friend Janie came here last year. She was supposed to come with me, but she went to Europe instead," April explained.

"Well, I'm glad you're here!" Karen said, smiling. "I'm in this cabin, too. We can both bunk on the sleeping porch. You'll love it here. Jackie's our counselor and she's great."

"I know. I met her a little while ago."

"Come on! I'll show you around!" Karen said, as she took April's sleeping bag from her.

Cabin One was a narrow building with a wooden floor, unfinished walls, and exposed rafters. To April, it looked like a tight fit for the six girls who were depositing their bags in whatever space they could find.

"Out here!" Karen called, dragging April's sleeping bag onto the porch out back. Completely screened in, it projected over the incline behind the cabin. Three sets of bunks and three battered dressers nearly filled the whole space.

April looked up at the clear plastic ceiling. "This is *really* sleeping under the stars!"

"It's kind of cramped, but with the plastic roof it doesn't feel that way." Karen pointed to a lower bunk. "The top one's mine. Why don't you dump your stuff here?"

"Who else is bunking out here?" April asked, as she put her belongings down.

"Sandra Parker from the music department

at school, two girls from Wellington, and one from Garden Grove," Karen answered.

Knowing there was a third girl from Spring Valley High raised April's spirits. She shoved her suitcase under the bunk and hung her garment bag on a nail sticking out of a two-by-four. Finding a spot for her guitar case proved more difficult, so she shoved it under the bed with the suitcase. *I wonder if I should have bothered to lug it up here,* she thought. *I probably won't play it at all.*

"Why don't you unpack later, after you have your voice audition?" Karen suggested.

"Tell me about the audition," April said, feeling those butterflies again. "What do we have to do?"

"Oh, it's easy. They'll tell you what to sing so they'll know what section to put you in. And they want to know how well you read music."

April made a face.

"Don't worry." Karen grabbed April's arm and hurried her along. "You'll do fine, I just know it!"

Half an hour later, April came out of the rec hall where the voice auditions had been held and found Karen leaning against the porch railing. "I'm hoping you're a second soprano like me," Karen said.

April shook her head. "No, I'm an alto."

Karen shrugged. "Guess we can't luck out

with everything." She led the way to the top of a large amphitheater that seemed to have been carved out of the hillside. A roof supported by posts and beams covered it completely.

"This is the Choir Bowl," Karen explained. "We have all our full rehearsals and concerts here."

April liked the idea of rehearsing outside. Hearing music, she looked down into the Bowl. On the patio, three girls were leaning over a piano while a guy pounded out a melody. It was the same good-looking guy she'd seen at registration! As he looked up from the keys, his dark eyes met April's. He grinned and winked.

April felt her pulse quicken, and she knew that the color was creeping into her cheeks. *I wonder if he can see how red I am,* she thought. Turning to Karen, she asked casually, "Who's the pianist?"

"That's Todd Barrett. He's been coming here for years. I'll introduce you later. First, let's finish with all this required junk."

April hated to leave, but Todd had gone back to playing the piano and smiling up at the girls. They couldn't seem to take their eyes off him. She tried to remember Todd from Janie's camp picture she'd looked at so often. Reluctantly she followed Karen to find out what she had to do next.

April had trouble concentrating during the

short test that would determine how much she knew about music and which theory class she'd be in. As she struggled to write down the notes the instructor played, she kept picturing the handsome, sandy-haired piano player named Todd who had winked at her.

Again Karen had waited for her. "How'd you do?" she asked.

April grimaced. "Awful! They probably think I'm tone-deaf."

Karen laughed. "No way! Come on, let's go finish unpacking."

As they went down the steps to their cabin, April thought only about seeing Todd again. Suddenly camp was beginning to look a lot more interesting!

Chapter Two

After supper, April walked with Karen and Sandy down the path to the Choir Bowl.

"I can't wait to see who else is back this year," Karen said, quickening her steps.

When they entered the Bowl, April immediately saw Todd sitting beside an auburn-haired boy whose face glowed with sunburn. April suddenly felt breathless. How could seeing a boy she didn't even know do this to her? Several other kids stood around Todd and the other boy, talking animatedly. As April watched, Todd suddenly glanced up and their eyes met the same way they had earlier that day. He gave her a quizzical look and grinned before someone asked him a question and he turned back to the group.

How embarrassing, April thought. He had caught her watching him twice!

A bell rang, and April heard several counselors calling, "Assembly time!"

She, Karen, and Sandy found seats together. "We have assembly after lunch and supper every day," Karen explained. "It's mainly for announcements and stuff. After this, we have evening rehearsal."

A white-haired man stepped to the middle of the Choir Bowl. He introduced himself as Mr. Collins, the camp director, and began a welcome speech.

"Mr. Collins started the camp ages ago," Karen whispered to her. "He's really cool."

April listened as he mentioned a few camp rules, shared some jokes and stories, and told them all to have fun. He then led some songs that everyone knew.

The evening rehearsal began after a short break. At this session they would find out what music they would sing for their concert. April felt excited, and only hoped it would be something she could handle.

A plump blonde woman who introduced herself as Mrs. Harper was the girls' chorus teacher. "This summer our musical director comes to us from London, England. Let's all welcome Mr. Paul Browning!" she announced proudly.

When the applause and chatter had stopped, Paul Browning started arranging everyone into their sections for the evening rehearsal. April went over to stand by Sandy with the altos. She noticed that Todd was one row ahead of her and a little to the left, with the tenors. She hadn't been this close to him before, and she admired the way his long-ish, tawny hair curled at the nape of his neck. April wondered what it would be like to touch those curls. The thought gave her goose bumps. If she felt this way just *looking* at him, how would she feel when she actually met him—if she even got to meet him?

After everyone had taken their seats, Paul beamed. "Jolly good!" he said in his clipped English accent, and then began handing out the music. April took one look at her copy and felt a sinking sensation in her stomach. The words were in Latin!

For the next hour and a half, April struggled with the difficult words, though she enjoyed the music. She was exhausted when Paul finally announced, "That's it for tonight!"

Everyone relaxed, and they all hurried off to the rec hall for a social hour of "get-acquainted games." April had been looking forward to this activity, hoping to get acquainted with one person in particular. Where was Todd, anyway? Then she saw him, surrounded by a crowd of guys and several girls at the far end of the room. If he was

15

always with a bunch of friends, how would she ever get to know him? Karen seemed to have forgotten her casual promise to introduce them.

Greg, a tall, blond counselor, yelled for everybody's attention, then instructed, "Make two circles, one inside the other, facing each other."

"Oh, good!" Karen said, laughing. "This is my favorite get-acquainted game." Greg explained that each person was to say his or her name and take a good look at the person in front of them before moving on to the next.

"Memorize those faces," Greg told the campers. "At least, try to remember *something* about them so you'll recognize them around camp. Jackie will play a chord on the piano every fifteen seconds, and that's when you'll move on."

April stared hard at the first person across from her as she gave her name. It was a girl named Alice who had been at April's table during supper. *Fifteen seconds doesn't sound like much, but it's a very long time to look at someone*, April thought. As the two circles began to move, April realized that Todd would soon be opposite her. Would he remember her? Would he wink at her again? And if he did, how should she react?

Sandy's familiar giggle brought April's attention back to the game, and fifteen seconds later she was looking into the dancing green eyes of Todd's sunburned friend, who told her his name was Jon. As April introduced herself, he wiggled his ears, and she couldn't help laughing.

Then she found herself facing Todd. April's breath caught in her throat as she looked up into his brown eyes. They were much darker than they had seemed from a distance. She guessed that he must be at least six inches taller than her own five feet five. He looked down at her and smiled as he said his name, and April felt herself melting. She could hardly remember her *own* name!

The circles moved again. How could she possibly have thought fifteen seconds seemed like a long time? While she was staring at Todd, the time had passed in a flash. What had he thought of her? *Oh, please let him remember me*, April begged silently.

After a few more games, everyone sang a few songs while two of the counselors accompanied them on guitars.

"You'll have to bring your guitar down for the singing sometime," Karen whispered to April.

"We'll see," she answered, hoping Karen wouldn't tell anyone she played the guitar. She'd have to practice a lot before she'd be comfortable playing in front of all these talented musicians.

At last Jackie glanced at her watch. "That's it for tonight, gang. The warning bell rings in five minutes."

"Let's find Sandy and head back to the cabin," Karen said. "Lights-out is ten-fifteen and that doesn't give us much time."

When they returned to the cabin with the others, April realized just how crowded the sleeping porch was with six girls getting ready for bed at the same time. *Crowded, but fun*, she thought as she unrolled her sleeping bag and shook it to fluff up the down filling.

Jackie poked her head in from the main cabin. "Glad you're in Cabin One, April. You seem to fit right in."

April grinned. "Thanks. So far everything's been fine," she said, and looked at Karen.

"Great. Goodnight," Jackie said, smiling at the girls.

As Jackie went back inside, April climbed into her sleeping bag and rubbed her feet together to warm them up. It had gotten surprisingly cold after the sun went down. She snuggled deeper into her bag, listening to the happy voices all around her and enjoying the easy banter. Her cabinmates were really nice—Karen was so friendly, always smiling, with a warmth that made April feel she'd known her forever. April was sure she'd enjoy living with all of them. Maybe she'd even learn to be more relaxed and easygoing herself.

The sound of a piano drifted to April's ears a moment later, followed by a sweet soprano voice singing a folk ballad.

"What's that?" she asked Karen in the bunk above.

Karen leaned over the side. "Every night we have Slumber Music right before taps. Sometimes it's a solo, sometimes a duet, or even just an instrumental. Anybody can volunteer."

What a fantastic way to end the day, April thought. There was so much talent here that they'd probably never run out of volunteers, though she was sure she'd never be confident enough to be one of them.

When the last notes of the song died away, Karen leaned over again to whisper, "Did you bring any sheet music with you?"

"Not much. Just 'The Rose' and a couple of other things."

"I think 'The Rose' is one of the songs we're doing in Girls' Chorus for the concert this year. If there's a solo, you should try out," Karen said.

"Oh, I couldn't," April murmured. The very thought of singing a solo made her cringe.

"I'd love to sing a duet with you for Slumber Music," Karen continued, "but Sandy and I planned to sing together even before we got here."

April couldn't help feeling a little disappointed. A solo was out of the question, but it might have been fun to sing a duet with her new friend.

She closed her eyes, listening as taps was played on a French horn from somewhere in the distance. April had never heard it played on anything but a trumpet before. She wondered if Todd was listening, too. And most of all, she wondered if he would remember her tomorrow.

Chapter Three

April stretched lazily in the warm sun as she half dozed among several other campers by the side of the pool, enjoying the luxury of doing absolutely nothing. How glorious it was just to lie here, soaking up the rays after spending the morning adjusting to the camp routine.

Cabin cleanup and inspection had followed breakfast, and then the campers had all gathered above the Choir Bowl for flag raising. At Girls' Chorus rehearsal April had discovered that the music and the words were actually easier than at choir the night before. She even became so involved that she temporarily forgot about Todd!

Where was he now? April wondered. Getting to her feet, she adjusted the straps of her new black bathing suit with the bright red, orange, and yellow stripes. She'd thought he'd definitely be at the pool during free time since the afternoon had turned so warm and sunny.

Putting her sunglasses and sunscreen in her tote bag, April wrapped her towel around her waist and wandered down past the dining hall and over to the bulletin board that announced coming events. Seeing the sign-up sheet for the moonlight hike that was to take place that night, she scanned the list for Todd's name. There it was—he was going! On impulse, April added hers to the bottom of the list right under Karen's.

She might just get up the nerve to talk to Todd on the hike. And if she did, who knew what might happen as they walked through the woods in the light of the moon?

That night after rehearsal, April changed clothes three times before deciding on jeans and a bright yellow sweatshirt for the hike. She gave her hair a final brushing, grabbed her flashlight, and hurried to the meeting spot on the porch of the rec hall.

A lot of kids were gathered there, but where was Karen? She hadn't seen her since rehearsal.

"Oh, no!" she moaned as Karen suddenly appeared out of the dark and walked onto

22

the well-lit porch. She was dressed in jeans and a bright yellow sweatshirt, too! "We look like twins!"

"Tweedledum, meet Tweedledee!"

How embarrassing, April thought. *Everyone will think we planned it this way.* But there was no time to change.

Suddenly she heard laughter behind her. Turning, she saw Todd standing with Jon.

"Oh, I hope they're not laughing at us," April said, half aloud and half to herself.

"Huh?" Karen gave her a puzzled look.

"Nothing," April said sighing, wondering how Karen could be so unconcerned with their identical attire.

Todd looks so nice, she thought, in his white sweatshirt and faded Levi's. The white shirt would make it easy to keep track of him in the dark.

One of the counselors arrived, handed each camper an orange for a snack, and gave brief directions. Then the group started across camp to pick up the trail behind the boys' cabins. Flashlights bobbed along, lighting the path ahead and occasionally a treetop or a laughing face. Loud voices and giggling sent advance warnings of their approach to any wildlife in the woods ahead. Deep pine needles made the trail spongy, like walking on a foam mattress. The moon was rising, and brilliant stars sparkled in the sky, helping to light the way.

Someone ahead started singing, and as the melody made its way down the line of campers strung out on the trail, everyone joined in. They were soon singing in four-part harmony, and the simple song became a lovely blending of voices. Other songs followed, and April relaxed as she sang the alto line, forgetting about everything except the beauty of the music and the jeweled sky.

The songs dwindled away as the trail toughened. April concentrated on where she put her feet on the root-covered path—she certainly didn't want to fall flat on her face like a real klutz. They started to climb, and she began to puff, admitting to herself that she was a little out of shape.

"We'll be coming to a grassy area soon. That's where we'll rest," Karen assured her.

April realized she had no idea where they were going. When she had signed up for the hike, it was Todd's name rather than the destination that had been the important thing. *I wonder where Todd is now?* she thought, trying to locate his white sweatshirt.

Suddenly a flashlight shone in April and Karen's faces, lighting up their identical yellow shirts. "What have we here? The Bobbsey Twins?" the voice from behind the light called out. April raised her own flashlight and saw Todd's friend Jon. So he *had* noticed their clothes, after all.

"Well, I don't like to break up a matching

set, but it seems to me you two could use some company," Jon said. He slipped between them and linked his arms in theirs.

As they tramped up the trail together joking around, laughing, and talking, April soon noticed the easy banter between Karen and Jon.

When they reached the level area, they all collapsed on the ground, laughing and gasping for breath. Jon held his aching sides, and Karen and April wiped tears of mirth from their eyes as the other campers flopped down on the grass around them.

"What's so funny?" Todd asked, shining his flashlight on the three of them.

"I guess you had to be there," Jon explained, motioning for Todd to join them. "Pull up a rock and sit down."

Grinning, Todd found himself a seat. He looked straight at April. "You're April Sullivan, right? What's a nice girl like you doing hanging out with these two clowns?"

April could hardly believe it. There Todd sat, actually talking to her. And he remembered her name! She tried to say something witty, but nothing came out, so she just smiled at him. *How could I be such a jerk?* she thought. What was he thinking of her now? Probably that she was a complete loser for not saying anything.

Todd turned to the others. "How do you like the hike so far?"

"Very amusing," Karen said, grinning at Jon.

"Jon's great entertainment, especially when he has an appreciative female audience." Todd looked back at April, studying her for a minute. "Are you okay?"

"It's—the altitude. I'm not used to hiking at six thousand feet." That was only part of it, but April hoped he would accept her excuse. She certainly couldn't let him know the effect he had on her.

"It takes a little getting used to, and then you'll be ready for Happy Gap."

"What's that?" April asked.

Todd leaned back to look up at the stars. "It's a place in those large rocks behind the campfire circle. But it's a lot steeper climb and it's never done at night."

"Give me your oranges, girls," Jon broke in, reaching for the fruit. He added his own and began juggling all three at once.

"Hey! You're good!" Karen cried with enthusiasm.

"Better believe it," Jon said smugly. "And I have many other hidden talents which I just may reveal to you someday."

Todd gave April a nudge to get her attention, putting his finger to his lips. Standing up, he tiptoed behind Jon, who was too absorbed in his juggling act to notice. As April watched, he reached out suddenly, jabbing Jon in the ribs.

"Argh!" Jon buckled over in surprise, the

oranges flying in three directions. Laughing, April retrieved hers as Jon tackled Todd. The two exploded in gasping bursts of laughter and collapsed back on the ground while the other campers cheered.

April knew Jon was showing off for someone, but she didn't think it was for her—Todd would be her choice, anyway.

Several campers drifted over to sit with them. A slim girl with a long, dark braid perched herself next to Todd and started whispering to him. It was the same girl who had snubbed April at registration.

He doesn't seem to mind at all, April thought. She resented the easy conversation between them, especially since April had blown her opportunity to talk to him.

The general conversation turned to upcoming activities and last season's parties and concerts. "Remember the big dance we had last year?" asked the girl with the braid.

"Do I ever," Jon said, winking. "You were the belle of the ball, Connie."

Todd smiled at her, and Connie leaned closer to him.

April felt a stab of jealousy. What had happened at that dance? Maybe Connie and Todd were an item, though she hadn't seen them together before tonight. Everyone started talking about other parties at camp while April said nothing.

"We'll have dances and parties this year

too, April," Karen said, noticing her friend's silence. "The first dance is a week from Saturday night."

April appreciated Karen's attempt to include her, but she felt like an outsider again. Nobody but Karen seemed to care about her at all.

April recognized Greg, the counselor who led the "get-acquainted games," when he came over and announced, "We'll be starting back down in about five minutes." He sat on a rock beside Jon, and everyone quieted down. Only the rustle of a breeze in the branches overhead and the occasional hoot of an owl disturbed the stillness.

Then Greg stood and started down the trail, with the others straggling behind. The moon rose high in the sky, surrounded by millions of stars.

"Pretty, isn't it?" Todd said, falling in step next to April.

She smiled, surprised and pleased that he was walking with her, and not Connie. "It reminds me of a scene in a movie I saw a long time ago," she said. "A jewel thief poured a pouchful of diamonds onto a black velvet cloth. That's what the sky looks like to-night."

"You're right—it does," he agreed. "Hey! Do you write? You know, poems and songs and stuff?"

"No," she said. "What made you ask?"

Todd shrugged. "Oh, I don't know. Maybe what you just said about the sky. It sounded sort of poetic."

April was amazed. Todd actually thought she might be a poet, and all she'd done was tell him about an old movie! "Do *you* write poems?" she asked.

"I write songs, but I have a lot more luck with the music than I do the lyrics."

"I'm sure they're just great!" Oh, why did she have to gush like that?

"Well, it's just a hobby, but someday I'd like to sell some of them."

"I'm sure you will!" April said.

Todd seemed pleased by her enthusiasm. Suddenly he pointed to the sky. "Look, do you see the Big Dipper?"

April searched until she made out the bright stars of the constellation. "Yes, there it is."

"The two stars in the front of the dipper point to the North Star," he explained.

April really didn't care which stars pointed where, as long as Todd stayed near her. As she tried to snap out of her dreamy haze and think of a clever comment to keep Todd's interest, she forgot to keep the beam of her flashlight on the path. Without warning, her foot caught on a root and she pitched forward, lurching into Todd. *Oh great*, she thought, *now he's* really *going to think I'm clumsy!* But he quickly reached out and

29

grabbed her elbow, helping her regain her balance.

"Thanks," she murmured, very much aware of the touch of his hand.

They walked without speaking now, and Todd continued to hold April's arm, as if to make sure she didn't fall again. Surprised at the comfortable silence between them, she made no attempt at conversation. Soon they reached the outskirts of camp.

At the point where the boys left the group and headed for their cabins, Todd let go of her arm. "See ya!" he said as he ran to catch up with Jon.

See ya, she echoed silently. Yes, she would see him at every rehearsal, at every activity. She'd see him when he was too busy to see her. She'd see him when she closed her eyes each night and when she opened them each morning.

"See you in my dreams," she said softly, gazing up at the star-spangled sky.

Karen had walked back with Jon. Now she caught up with April. "Well?" she asked, looking at April inquisitively. "Don't you have something to share?"

April sighed. "Isn't Todd just heavenly?"

"Looks to me like *you're* the heavenly one— your head's in the clouds," Karen teased.

"Oh, Karen, do you think he likes me?" April hugged herself, closing her eyes. Karen was right. Her head was in the clouds and if someone didn't hold her down, she might drift away.

Karen laughed. "I didn't know you were that interested or I'd have left you two alone sooner."

Chapter Four

Midmorning the next day, April, Karen, and Sandy hurried to the Girls' Chorus rehearsal. April hadn't been able to eat any breakfast and she was afraid her grumbling stomach would be out of harmony with the music.

Holding up her hand to quiet the chattering girls, Mrs. Harper began the session with an announcement. "As I believe I mentioned, 'The Rose' will be one of our selections for the final concert, along with a medley of three Hungarian folk songs." She brushed her hand through her short blond hair and took off her glasses, looking out over the girls in front of her. "What you don't know," she continued, "is that there will be two solos, one in the second folk song and one at the beginning of 'The Rose.' I'll hold auditions next week after we've rehearsed and everyone is familiar with the music. I hope you'll all consider trying out."

April caught her breath. "The Rose" was one of her favorite songs. She had even sung it several times before. But then again, she'd only sung for her friends, not in front of a huge audience of strangers.

During rehearsal, April imagined herself singing the solo, finishing to thunderous applause, and graciously taking a bow. In her daydreams she was calm and confident. But when she came back to reality and pictured all those people sitting there staring at her, she knew she'd never be able to do it. There was no use even auditioning.

On the way to lunch with Karen and Sandy, April asked if either of them planned to try out.

"Not me!" Sandy said. "I don't want all those extra practices. There's enough to do already without using up more of my precious free time."

April turned to Karen. "How about you?"

Karen shook her head. "I'd like to, but I sang a solo in the final concert last year. They never use the same people two years in a row. You'll have to be our representative at the audition."

"No way! I'm not going to try out either,"

April said firmly. "Big crowds terrify me. I'd never be able to sing a note."

"Well, think about it. You've got until next week," Karen said.

When they reached the dining hall, April looked around the room for Todd. As usual, she found him and Jon in the middle of a group of campers. Todd was entertaining while trying to eat a large submarine sandwich. Except for last night, she'd never seen him without a group of kids around. There were no empty seats at his table, and even if there had been, she doubted she'd have the courage to join them. Todd might wonder what she was doing there or what she wanted. Maybe last night hadn't been as special for him as it had for her. A little disappointed, April joined Karen, Sandy, and some other girls at another table.

After lunch and all-camp rehearsal, April started back to the cabin for rest hour. She didn't feel like hanging out and talking to people. Lost in her thoughts, she didn't see her counselor until she almost walked into her.

"Don't mow me down!" Jackie cried, laughing.

"Sorry," April said. "We missed you on the hike last night."

Jackie made a face. "I had to stay down here to keep an eye on the kids who didn't go. Duty calls."

"Where are you going?" April asked.

"To pick up my mail," she answered.

"Oh, I forgot about mail! Where do we get it? Is there a post office here at camp?"

Jackie motioned for April to join her. "I'll show you where it is."

The girls walked over to the main building, where a peeling metal table stood in one corner of the porch. Dozens of letters were spread across it.

Jackie pointed to the table. "There's our post office! Not much mail today, but give it a week and there'll be tons. Here's Cabin One's pile. Just dig through and see if there's anything for you."

April saw that she had no letters. She waited while Jackie sorted through the mail and slipped an envelope into her shorts pocket.

"C'mon, let's head back," Jackie said, as they walked toward the cabin. "Do you like it here so far?"

"It's great!" April replied, thinking of Todd.

"I love it here," Jackie said. "It's one of the few music camps where the counselors get to participate in the rehearsals and performances." They reached the steps to the cabin. "You look kind of beat. Why don't you go catch a few winks so you'll enjoy the rest of your free time?"

April collapsed onto her bunk, glad for the opportunity to relax. Rest hour had seemed silly when she'd first heard about it, like nap time in kindergarten. She hadn't realized then how busy the campers would be and how much they would need this quiet time.

Sinking deep into her pillow, she decided to try to think of ways to attract Todd's attention. But before she could come up with anything, she fell asleep, too tired for any new schemes.

Voices awakened April about an hour later as the other girls climbed off their bunks and began getting into swimsuits, chattering about how they were going to spend their free time until supper.

Karen leaned over from her top bunk, hanging upside down above her friend. "April, are you awake?"

April giggled. "With you dangling there like some kind of oversized bat, I may still be asleep and having a nightmare!"

"Are you going to the pool?" Karen asked as she flipped down to the floor.

"Maybe later. I thought I'd play my guitar a little. I'll come up in a while."

"Okay, but don't wait too long. It starts to cool off pretty fast," Karen advised. She pulled on a blue-and-black bikini that looked great with her golden tan. Then she saluted April, grabbed a towel, and ran out of the cabin.

As the screen door banged shut behind the last girl, April lay on her bunk for a moment, savoring the silence. It was nice to be alone for a change.

She rolled off her bed and dragged out her guitar case from beneath it.

Strumming the familiar chords made her remember how many times she had withdrawn to her own bedroom at home and played when things got tough, or she felt sad or lonely. The music usually made her feel much better. *I wonder if Todd ever writes songs for a guitar,* she thought, trying to imagine the kind of music he wrote.

The sounds of the piano from the patio intruded on her quiet, so she returned the guitar to its padded case and pushed it under the bunk. She tied her hair back with a blue ribbon that matched her shorts, took one last look in the cracked mirror, and hurried down the cabin steps toward the patio in front of the Choir Bowl.

Todd was sitting at the upright piano, pounding out a melody and adding variations as he improvised, while half a dozen campers, mostly girls, hung over the top and sang along. April hesitated, then walked toward the group.

"Over here, April," Sandy called, motioning to a spot next to her.

Relieved to see her friend, April joined Sandy and watched Todd's nimble fingers dance over the keys to produce an upbeat melody. Glancing up, she found him looking at her. "What took you so long to get here?" Todd asked as he smiled at her.

April felt her face getting warm and was sure it matched his red shirt. Why did she always have to blush like that? She was glad he noticed she was there.

They sang for almost an hour before Todd struck a final chord and announced that the session was over. Shoving back the bench, he stood up.

"Time for a Popsicle break!" he announced. "Anyone else interested?"

"Me!" shouted a short, blond girl. She came around the piano to join Todd, and they headed in the direction of the Snack Shack that was always open during free time. Turning back, he called, "See you tonight."

Was he talking to me? April asked herself, astonished. It *looked* as if he was, but she couldn't really tell. She stared after him as he and the blonde walked away. Should she have gone too? April wondered.

Sandy looked inquiringly at April. "Do you and Todd have something planned for tonight?"

Still gazing after Todd, April shook her head. Then from the path above the Choir Bowl she saw Connie, the girl with the long, dark braid, come down the steps, waving at Todd. She ran over to him and he slid one arm around each girl as they moved out of sight. April felt as if her heart had just sunk to the bottom of her stomach, and wondered if she looked as miserable as she felt. Trying to keep her voice calm, she said, "Connie and Todd seem to be pretty tight."

Sandy shrugged. "*Connie* wishes they were. She'll try anything to get Todd." Sandy kicked a stone, then glanced at April. "Do you like him?"

April felt herself blushing again. "Well, I . . ."

"I don't blame you," Sandy said. "And don't worry about Connie. She's been after him for a couple of years, and she hasn't caught him yet."

There's always a first time, April thought, wishing Todd's arm was around *her* waist and she were the one going with him to buy Popsicles.

After evening rehearsal, April lingered in the Choir Bowl, stacking her music neatly in the rack. Todd had said nothing further about seeing her, and nothing special had been planned for tonight's recreation period, so she intended to join Karen and Sandy in the rec hall.

"Hi!"

Taken by surprise, she turned to see Todd and Jon standing right behind her.

"We didn't mean to scare you," Todd said, grinning at her. "Want to play Ping-Pong? Jon and I need some new competition."

April laughed. "I'm not very good, but I'll take you on."

They walked up to the nurse's office where a Ping-Pong table was set up on the lighted porch under the overhanging roof.

April picked up a paddle. "Who do I get to play first?"

"Me!" Todd said, grabbing the other paddle.

Jon pulled up a folding chair. "I'll referee," he said.

"Watch out for wild shots," Todd warned April as he prepared to serve.

"Mine or yours?" she retorted, amazed that she actually cracked a joke, and feeling as much at ease as if she'd known him for years. Maybe she was finally getting over her shyness in talking to boys.

After April lost by a narrow margin, Jon took the paddle from Todd. "Now that you've worn her down, I'll finish her off."

"Oh, yeah? We'll see about that!" April teased.

"Watch out for his spin serve," Todd told her.

"No fair coaching!" Jon complained. "Whose side are you on, anyway?"

"The winning side, I hope," Todd remarked.

April laughed, and Jon grimaced at her. "This is no laughing matter! My honor as a Ping-Pong pro is at stake. On with the game!"

At game point with April leading, she hit a soft shot to the corner that Jon couldn't reach. He sprawled across the table, moaning, "Oh, the agony of defeat!"

Todd grabbed April's hand and waved it in the air. "The winner and new champion!"

The warmth of his hand clasping hers sent a tingle through April, and she was sorry when he let her go.

Todd looked at Jon, who squared his shoulders in mock seriousness. "I am forced to retire in disgrace." He bowed to April. "I hope I may have the honor of a rematch."

"Let's go sit on the patio," Todd suggested when Jon had gone.

April's pulse raced. He obviously wanted to be alone with her, and she definitely wanted a chance to be alone with him!

They sat down on one of the benches along the edge of the patio outside the main building, where several other couples were talking quietly. Piano music drifted through the night from the rec hall up the hill. It was a perfect setting for romance.

Todd pointed to the starry sky. "There's the Big Dipper again."

"I see it," April said.

"You can usually find the Big Dipper wherever you are." Todd leaned against the back of the bench. "Sometimes I can see it from my bedroom window at home."

"Where do you live?" April asked.

"Tustin," he answered. "How about you?"

"Spring Valley. That's only about twenty minutes away from Tustin."

"There are quite a few of us here from Orange County," Todd said.

Then they sat together in silence. April was thrilled just being close to him, and when her arm brushed his, a jolt of electricity raced through her. *I should be making some great conversation,* she thought. She felt so nervous about what would happen next, but when she glanced at Todd, he smiled assuringly at her and reached over to entwine his fingers with hers.

His touch made April's heart beat wildly. She wished she dared to snuggle closer to him, and that this wonderful moment would last forever.

But it didn't.

Todd released her hand. "It won't be long until lights-out, and I have to make a phone call," he said.

April nodded, unable to think of anything to say that wouldn't reveal her disappointment. She felt empty. All of the excitement his nearness had generated was suddenly gone. Did she mean anything to him at all? Or would he latch on to a different girl tomorrow? He seemed to enjoy being with her, and even told Jon to go away tonight so they could be alone together. Surely that meant something.

April stood up after Todd left. She really should call home, too. Her mom and dad would be eager to hear how she was doing. But she didn't want to run into Todd—she certainly didn't want him to think she had followed him. By the time she walked to where the phone booths were located, she figured that Todd would be finished.

When she reached the phones, however, Todd was still on the line, his handsome profile clearly visible in the lighted booth. Who could he be talking to for so long?

April heard him laugh, obviously enjoying his conversation. *He wouldn't talk this long to his parents,* she thought. *I wonder if it's a girl?*

Just then she heard him say, "I sure wish you were here, Nancy. I really miss you."

April froze. Todd had a girlfriend back home!

Chapter Five

April stepped into a vacant booth next to Todd's and wondered if she could dial in the dark to avoid having the light come on when she shut the door. Then she decided that was silly. She slammed the door behind her, blinking as light flooded the tiny cubicle. When Todd looked up and waved, April acknowledged him and deposited her money.

After three rings her father answered. At the sound of his voice, April found herself feeling homesick. After all, she hadn't been away from home this long since her freshman class trip.

"Hi, honey. How's my camper?" he asked in the warm, deep voice she loved so much.

"I'm great," April replied, swallowing the

lump in her throat. "They really keep us busy—I've hardly had time to breathe."

"How's the music? As much fun as you thought it would be?"

"Some of the words are in Latin," she groaned. "It's easier now, but that first night— yuck!"

Mr. Sullivan laughed. "If I don't let your mother talk, she's going to burst."

April braced herself for questions she knew would be coming. Then she heard her mother's voice bubbling over the line. "Hi, April. Are you all settled? Have you made a lot of new friends?"

Friends, April thought. *The first thing she says. Always friends. As if having friends could solve every problem!* Well, maybe for her mother, it did. "I'm having a blast!" she exaggerated, hoping to avoid more questioning.

Mrs. Sullivan breathed a relieved sigh. "So everyone turned out to be friendly?"

"Karen Sanchez and I are bunkmates. And Sandy Parker from school is in our cabin, too."

"I'm so glad. I told you everything would be fine. Nothing much is new here—Danny and Tim say 'Hi.' "

"Well, I should go," April said. "I have to be in my cabin by lights-out, and that'll be any minute now."

"I'm glad you called. Remember, you can call collect anytime. We love you, honey," Mrs. Sullivan said before she hung up.

April hung up still feeling a little homesick. She stepped out of the phone booth, and noticed that the one next to hers was dark.

A few days later after lunch, April descended the steps to the Choir Bowl for assembly, looking for a place to sit in the sun. "Assembly time!" a deep male voice yelled. "Hurry and get a seat!"

A short, dark-haired counselor was impatiently hustling everyone into chairs, glowering as the kids sauntered in at a casual pace.

"There you are." Karen sat down beside her. "Wonder what thrilling announcements we'll hear today?"

April moved over to give Karen more room. "Do you know when we go to Lake Arrowhead?"

"I think it's next week—probably Friday." Karen slid down in her seat and rested her legs on the seat of the chair in front of her. "What's with Roger today?"

"Is that Roger?" April nodded at the counselor she'd been watching. "You got me. He's been yelling at everybody, but no one seems to pay any attention to him."

Karen laughed. "Oh, he's always in a snit about something."

April wanted to ask why, but Mr. Collins, the camp director, began the announcements. "The photographer will arrive at four o'clock this afternoon to take the camp picture," he said.

April's mind wandered back to the many

times she and Janie had pored over the camp pictures from past years. This year, she would be in the picture, and so would Todd.

After several more announcements, the campers were excused. April yawned, thinking that Music Appreciation had better feature some really loud selections, or she'd soon be fast asleep.

At three forty-five that afternoon, the sleeping porch of Cabin One was littered with discarded clothes. T-shirts, jeans, and shorts lay tangled on the bunks or draped over posts. Wet bathing suits and damp towels sagged from a clothesline strung from one end of the porch to the other. Makeup and hair dryers crowded dresser tops as all six girls finished their last-minute preparations for the camp picture.

"The bathroom's jammed," Karen announced, struggling into a hot pink T-shirt as she came out to the porch. "Believe it or not, we're better off in here."

April wedged herself between two other girls, trying to peek into the room's only mirror. "I just want to get *one* look," she pleaded. She scowled at the freckles across the bridge of her nose. There had to be at least a dozen new ones. Quickly she applied pink lip gloss, dug a comb out from under a pile of socks and ran it through her hair, then moved away to make room for Sandy, who was bouncing up and down impatiently.

"Hurry up, girls. The photographer's here!" Jackie yelled from the cabin door.

"Welcome to the zoo!" Karen yelled back.

Jackie stepped onto the porch and made a face at the mess. "I see what you mean," she said. "Just leave it for now. Come on, everybody. Roger Schwartz is in charge of this event, and he'll have my head if my group's late."

"Let's show them what hot chicks really look like," shouted one of the girls, and everybody poured out of the cabin, heading for the area outside the nurse's cabin where the photographs would be taken.

When they arrived, most of the other campers were already there. April noticed that the Riverside Madrigal Singers were all wearing their matching T-shirts. She couldn't help feeling glad that she and Karen were *not* doing their Bobbsey Twins routine this time.

"April!"

She turned to see Todd calling her over, and hurried to his side.

"Want to stand by me in the picture?" he asked, smiling down at her.

Do I want to? What a question! April thought. She just smiled back at him. "Sure—why not?" she answered casually.

Todd draped his arm over her shoulder and led her to the middle of a bunch of kids. "Third row, center. The best spot."

April wondered if anyone had seen Todd summon her. She hoped some of the kids

49

had noticed, especially Connie. For a few minutes at least, April could pretend that she was Todd's girl. She shivered with excitement and her smile widened.

Todd poked her in the ribs. "You don't have to grin until the photographer says 'cheese.' "

April giggled, realizing that she'd been standing there grinning like an idiot.

Todd laughed, too, and squeezed her shoulders. Together they watched the counselors climb up to the roof of the nurse's cabin and sit along the edge to form the top row of the picture. Roger directed the action as he had at assembly.

"Greg, zip up your jacket . . . slide forward, Julie," he ordered.

The moment he saw Jackie, he screamed, "Jackie, where's your Bear Mountain jacket? You have to look like all the other counselors!"

Todd shook his head. "Roger thinks he's so cool. Give him one little job and he thinks he's Camp Dictator."

"Friend of yours?" April asked, raising her eyebrows.

"Unfortunately, he's my counselor," Todd told her. "Last year he was just a camper, but this year he's graduated to the staff, and it's gone to his head."

"Chill out, Rog." Jackie moved toward the edge of the roof. "I'll climb down and get the jacket."

"I'll get it!" April called up to her, and dashed off.

I have to be crazy to be doing this, she thought. Todd had asked her to stand next to him for the picture and here she was, running off. But Jackie had always been so nice to her. . . .

April found Jackie's windbreaker on one of the bunks in Cabin One, rushed back up the hill, and tossed the jacket up to her counselor.

"Thanks, April! I owe you one," Jackie said.

April looked around to find Todd, and froze when she saw Connie standing next to him with her arm wrapped around his waist. Connie's triumphant smirk told April she had no intention of moving. Todd motioned for her to come to his other side, but April shook her head, biting her lip to hold back the tears. Her special time with Todd was all ruined. She'd actually spoiled it herself by doing something for Jackie.

Just as she decided to go stand on the far edge of the group, someone reached out and grabbed her hand. It was Jon. He got down on one knee and begged dramatically, "May I have the pleasure of standing next to you in the picture?"

April glanced over at Todd, who looked puzzled. Connie just smiled and snuggled closer to him. That did it.

51

"Terrific!" April said to Jon, forcing a big phony smile.

Jon got to his feet and, taking her hand, dragged her over to the group, squeezing between people until they were standing beside Todd and Connie. Todd leaned over to say something to Jon but before he could, Roger hollered for quiet, standing on a chair and waving his arms. When the chatter died down, he introduced the photographer, then climbed on the roof to take his place with the other counselors.

The photo session didn't take long. As soon as it was over, the campers scattered in different directions for the rest of their free time. But with Jon's arm still around her waist and Todd's arm draped over Jon's shoulder, April couldn't move. She wondered if they would remain a threesome forever. Oh, no—a foursome. How could she forget Connie, still clutching Todd from his other side?

No way would April spend her free time with Connie hanging on to Todd. She broke their chain, muttering, "Thanks for the picture," and stalked away.

What a dumb thing to say, she thought. *Oh well, I don't feel very clever right now, anyway. Just when I think I've made some progress with Todd she comes pushing in and spoils it. Why doesn't she find some other guy?*

"April, wait up!" Todd called. "I want to talk to you."

Reluctantly, April waited for him to catch up to her. They walked along together, neither of them speaking. Finally, Todd reached out and took her elbow, turning her to face him. "Come on, April. What's wrong?"

"Nothing," she mumbled.

"If it's nothing, how come you latched on to Jon so fast the minute you came back? I thought you were going to stand near me in the picture."

April jerked her arm free. "So did I . . . but when I got back, you had somebody else with you."

"You mean Connie?" He laughed. "She's just a friend. She's been here at camp every year that I have."

April started walking again. How could a guy not notice that a girl was throwing herself at him? Did Todd actually believe Connie just wanted to be friends? Maybe guys really were naive about girls!

Realizing that Todd had stopped several yards behind her, April turned around. He shrugged. "I *was* going to ask if you wanted to hike up to Happy Gap, but if you're not interested . . . "

April didn't have to think twice. "I'm interested," she said with a shy smile.

Todd grinned. "Okay! The trail starts over here." He pointed in the direction of the boys' cabins.

For the next half hour the steep climb took all their attention. Todd held on to

April's hand, helping her up over the difficult places. When they reached the top, he led her over to a rocky crest where they could see the magnificent view. "I love it up here," he said.

"It's beautiful," April whispered, gazing at the panorama below them. This wonderful moment was like a dream. If she could only save it forever—the two of them on top of the world! She watched ripples chasing each other across a tiny lake. The sun made the water sparkle, and on the far side, dark green cedars and rugged boulders covered the side of the mountain. She glanced over at Todd and found him watching her. "I thought we were here to admire the scenery," she teased.

"I am." He moved closer, looking down at her.

April felt the warmth spread up her face. *There I go again! Why can't I just be cool?* she asked herself.

Todd touched her cheek. "You're cute when you blush," he said softly.

Now Todd rested his hands on her shoulders. April looked up and noticed the sun sparkling in his eyes and the wind playing with his hair. Suddenly she knew he was going to kiss her. What should she do? Though she longed for his kiss, she was afraid that her response would reveal how little experience she'd had kissing boys. Todd gently pulled her closer, and April slid into his arms. As he lowered his face to hers, "Hey! Anyone up there?" someone called out from just below the place where they were standing. Other voices started a camp song a little farther away.

April tried to pull back, but Todd held her tight, releasing her just as a group of kids came into sight with Jon in the lead. "Hey, you two. What's up?" Jon called.

"Perfect timing," Todd grumbled.

April was terribly embarrassed that they'd almost been seen. "Do you think they followed us?" she asked.

Todd shrugged, frowning. "I think Jon likes you, and he's just giving us a hard time."

That surprised April. Jon was awfully nice to her, but he was friendly with everyone. It pleased her that Todd didn't seem to like the idea. *I hope he's a little jealous,* April thought.

Before Jon and the others could join them, Todd said, "Let's get out of here." Taking April's hand, he led the way toward the trail back to camp.

April sighed. This had been such a wonderful day! Maybe not absolutely perfect since Jon and his crew had showed up at the wrong time, but Todd *had* been about to kiss her. That thought made her tingle all over. April wanted to enjoy that special sensation she'd felt in his arms again, and she could hardly wait for the dance next Saturday night.

Chapter Six

A week later, April, Karen, and Sandy wedged into a seat on one of the two old school buses that would take the campers to Lake Arrowhead. "This must be how sardines feel!" Karen giggled.

April squirmed, trying to get comfortable in her corner next to the window. "I'm glad it's a short ride."

"After we bounce along on this rickety bus, you'll think it has been *years*," Sandy said.

As the bus hit each rut in the bumpy dirt road, April held on to the window ledge to keep from falling into Sandy. But once they turned onto the highway, she was able to relax, and for the rest of the trip, she looked out the window and let her thoughts drift to Todd, who was on the other bus.

"Hey! Wake up!" Karen poked April to bring her out of her dreamworld as their bus entered Lake Arrowhead Village. April cried out in delight at the alpine-style buildings that lined the waterfront. "It's like a Swiss village!"

The minute the bus stopped, Karen sprang from her seat, followed by Sandy and April. They were the first to get out. "First stop same as usual?" Sandy asked, as the other campers took off in all directions.

"Absolutely!" Karen replied.

"Where are we going?" April asked.

"To McDonald's, of course."

McDonald's? April protested. "We came all this way to eat at McDonald's? And why are we eating now, anyway? We just had lunch an hour ago."

Karen rolled her eyes. "We *always* have two lunches when we come here—sometimes even two dinners!"

"It's our only chance to stock our poor deprived bods with junk food," Sandy added.

Shaking her head in amusement, April followed her friends down a narrow, winding street. "It's like being in another country," she exclaimed.

Karen and Sandy led the way down the street toward the lake, while April lagged behind to look in the windows of the quaint shops.

"Hurry, April, my stomach's having a Big Mac attack," Karen called over her shoulder, and April ran to catch up.

"Wow! This is one fancy McDonald's," she said, taking in the sunny deck with its view of the lake.

The girls placed their orders. Then, carrying trays loaded with sodas, fries, and hamburgers, they went out onto the deck.

Surprised to find that she was actually hungry, April ate quickly and looked out at the lake in front of them. A few sailboats and powerboats rippled the bright blue surface, and the wooded shore curtained the rim of the lake, parting occasionally to reveal summer cottages nestled among the trees.

In the marina close to them April could see a fleet of small rental boats bobbing along the dock, and some bumper boats bouncing on the ripples inside a square of rope and buoys.

"Hey! Look who's here!" Karen said suddenly, looking over the railing.

April looked, too, and saw Todd and Jon going out of a hardware store near the dock, carrying brown packages.

"If it isn't the gruesome twosome," Sandy called down to them as they approached, pretending to dump her tray on their heads.

"What's in the bags?" Karen asked, indicating the sacks they each carried.

"Vital equipment," Todd said mysteriously.

Jon grinned. "Top secret, not to be revealed under pain of death!"

Karen leaned over the railing. "Come on—

tell us! We know you're up to something sneaky."

"You better not ask any more questions," Jon advised solemnly. "We're innocent. It's just your suspicious minds."

"Will you get into trouble?" April asked.

"Trouble?" Jon and Todd repeated in unison. Jon looked at April with exaggerated shock. "What kind of trouble could two nice guys like us possibly get into?"

"Plenty!" Sandy rolled her eyes.

"Are you going to stay up there all day?" Todd asked.

Karen pulled April to her feet. "No way! We're going to show April the sights. How about you?"

"We're going back to the bus to stash this stuff. No sense dragging it around." Jon patted his bag.

"Maybe we'll see you later." Todd smiled at April. "We'll be down at the marina."

April smiled back at him. "Great!"

The three girls walked across the street to a gift shop. Wandering down the aisles, they poked through piles of souvenirs, read each other their favorite bumper stickers, and tried on all the sunglasses.

"Let's go look at books," Karen suggested. "I want to buy a teenage romance."

"I don't want to *read* about one, I want to *have* one!" Sandy exclaimed. She browsed through the rack of paperbacks, then showed

60

one to April. "Here, April—this one's called *Summer Romance*, and you're the only one who seems to have one going."

April laughed, blushing. "You can hardly call it a romance."

"Well it's certainly more than Karen or I have." Sandy sighed. "I wish I'd meet a special someone soon."

Karen shook her head and made a face. "The trouble is, we've known most of these guys for three years, and all the new ones are freshmen. Come on. Let's get out of here. We're missing prime sun time."

While Sandy went to check out the sports shop, April and Karen headed toward the marina. "I'm glad you decided to come in our bus instead of with Todd in the other one," Karen said with a smile.

"Me, too," April said. She didn't want to admit that Todd hadn't asked her to go with him. But it didn't matter because she was having a great time with Karen and Sandy. If Todd wanted to go off with Jon on some "secret mission," that was fine with her.

"Let's watch the water-skiers," Karen suggested.

April agreed. They walked out onto the dock. At the far end, they saw Todd and Jon leaning against the railing and strolled over to them. April promptly forgot about water-skiing when Todd said, "Want to rent a couple of bumper boats?"

"Let's do it!" Jon yelled, and they all raced to get their tickets. How would they split up, April wondered. Boy/boy, girl/girl, or boy/girl, boy/girl? She didn't have to worry. Todd linked elbows with her, pulling her to one of the bumper boats, which resembled two floating chairs mounted on huge inner tubes.

Todd took the wheel and they putted around the roped-off area. Suddenly, Jon and Karen's boat slammed into the back of theirs. "We'll get you for that!" Todd shouted, spinning the wheel to chase them. They were just about to crash into Jon and Karen, but a boat driven by a little boy zeroed in on them, knocking them into the float lines. "You try," Todd said, handing the wheel to April. She began to protest, but he took her hands and put them firmly on the wheel. Taking careful aim, she crashed into Jon and Karen.

"Good shot!" Todd called above the noise of the motors. "Look out! Here they come again!"

Now that April had gotten the hang of it, she was really enjoying herself, laughing and shrieking with the rest of them.

The ride was over too soon, and the attendant waved the boats over to the dock. Todd leapt out and reached down to help April. "You're a natural at this—a real maniac," he told her, grinning.

"You weren't so bad yourself," April laughed.

Jon and Karen came over to them. "We're going to go on the paddle wheeler. Want to come?" Karen asked.

"We'll have to hurry," Todd said. "It leaves on the hour."

The four ran for the ferry pier and managed to get tickets in the nick of time. Jon and Karen leaned over the rail up front, while Todd pulled April to the stern of the boat where they could watch the paddle wheel turn.

"The wheel's just for effect," Todd explained. "Actually there's an engine that powers the boat."

"Well, I'm going to pretend I don't know that," April said. "It's more romantic that way."

Todd smiled down at her. "Are you into romance?"

April didn't quite know what to say. She couldn't tell him that whenever she was with him, romance was always on her mind, so she said nothing.

Todd didn't ask again, but he put his arm around her as they gazed over the lake.

"Hey, there's a Hobie Cat!" April pointed to a catamaran skimming over the water. Two boys sat on the edge of the trampoline deck, leaning far out over the side.

Todd gripped her shoulder as the sailboat lifted up on one pontoon. "They're going over!"

April laughed. "No, they won't. It's supposed to do that. It's called 'flying a hull.' "

"How do you know so much about it?" Todd asked.

"We have a boat at home," April told him, then added impulsively, "You'll have to come sailing with us after camp."

Todd was silent for a moment, then said quietly, "Yeah . . ."

April suddenly felt the joy of the afternoon fade away. She had hoped that they might continue to see each other after the camp session was over, but she had also completely forgotten about Todd's "mystery phone girl." Whoever she was would surely reclaim him when he got home.

April was glad when Todd took a seat next to her on the bus for the trip back to camp, but as soon as the driver started the engine, he yawned and closed his eyes. Apparently romance wasn't on *his* mind. April closed her eyes, too, wishing she hadn't said anything about what might happen after camp. Obviously Todd was not interested. Why had she even mentioned it and ruined such a perfect day? She only hoped that she could make up for it at tomorrow night's dance.

Chapter Seven

On Saturday morning, April ran toward the dining hall. She had overslept, and now she was late for breakfast. Inside, the room buzzed with an unusual amount of conversation and laughter. April went unnoticed as she filled her plate and looked for Karen and Sandy. Suddenly, she heard Todd's name mentioned and strained to hear more, but it was just a jumble of noise.

Karen waved and April walked toward her, noticing the animated discussion at her table. She climbed over the bench and sat down between Karen and Sandy. "What's going on?"

"I *knew* they were up to something," Sandy said, giggling. "And those rats wouldn't let us in on it."

Karen was giggling, too. "They're such idiots."

"Will someone please tell me what's going on?" April demanded, turning from one girl to the other.

"Look over there." Karen pointed to the cleanup area, and April saw Jon and Todd behind the counter with large white aprons wrapped around their waists. Todd was wiping the surface of the counter with exaggerated care, and Jon whistled as he scraped dirty dishes. They both had mischievous grins on their faces and were well aware of the uproar. "Why are they on KP?" April asked.

Karen shrieked, "They painted Roger's feet *green* last night while he was asleep!"

"Oh my gosh!" April choked back her giggles, remembering the mysterious purchases the boys had made in the village last week. She looked over at Todd and when their eyes met, he saluted her. She waved back. "Where's Roger now?" she asked Karen.

Karen shrugged. "He came in, grabbed some cereal, and disappeared. He's never going to live this down!"

"Serves him right," Sandy said cheerfully, spreading peanut butter on her toast. "Roger's become a real jerk now that he's on staff."

"Yeah—he played tons of practical jokes when he was a camper," Karen added.

April shook her head. "Roger sure must be a sound sleeper. Hey, remember those packages? Think Todd and Jon got more than just paint?"

"Yeah, I wonder what else they're up to," Karen said.

When April had finished her breakfast, she carried her dishes over to the counter and set them down in front of Todd.

"Want to help?" he asked, grinning.

April laughed, shaking her head emphatically. "No, thanks. You're doing such a good job." Leaning over the counter, she whispered to both boys, "Got any more tricks up your sleeve?"

"Of course not," Todd said innocently and looked at Jon who just smiled.

April went back to sit at the table, where Karen and Sandy were still sipping their cocoa.

"Any explanation?" Sandy asked.

"No, but I can tell they're planning something."

"Great prank, huh?" said a voice behind April. She looked up to see Connie. Her dark eyes glinted hard when she looked at April. "Poor old Roger! I could hardly wait for everyone else to find out." She tossed her head, flipping her long braid over her shoulder, then returned to her own table.

April felt a twinge of jealousy. Had Connie known about the stunt? Could she have even helped Todd and Jon? Or did she just want April to think she had?

Outside, Karen stretched her arms above her head. "I hate to be stuck in rehearsal and waste all this sun, especially on Saturday!"

"At least there's the fifties dance tonight." April smiled as she thought of spending the evening with Todd.

Sandy sighed. "*You'll* have fun, but I think it'll be boring."

Karen poked Sandy. "What's with you today? You always liked dances before. Especially sock hops."

"I wish we could bring in some guys from town," Sandy answered. "I'll probably be stuck with one of those pimply freshmen!"

Absorbed in thoughts of the dance as she and her friends walked to the Choir Bowl, April wondered what she could wear that would look fifties-ish, and then tried to think of clever and romantic things she could say to Todd while they danced. When full camp rehearsal began, she reluctantly stopped daydreaming and instead looked for Todd.

He and Jon arrived halfway through rehearsal, and Todd dropped loudly into his metal chair. He looked angry as he flipped through the music to find his place.

I wonder what's happened to make him so mad, April mused. He certainly hadn't seemed upset earlier that morning on KP.

When rehearsal ended, April hurried to put her music away so she could catch Todd on her way to Music Theory class, but he hadn't waited for her. What could possibly be wrong?

April saw a group gathered around Jon, so she joined them to find out what was going on. "What happened to Todd?" she asked.

"Well, since you're all so concerned about *my* dilemma, I suppose I'll have to tell you," Jon said, pretending to be hurt.

April groaned. "Jon, just *tell us what happened.* Why is Todd so upset?"

"And what about me? Don't I look upset, too?" He gave them a sad puppy-dog look.

Karen ruffled his hair. "You're impossible!"

"Brace yourself, girls. I know this will come as a terrible shock, but my good friend Todd and I will not be attending the long-awaited dance this evening."

"You're kidding!" Sandy cried.

"What do you mean?" Karen demanded.

He dropped his playful tone. "We've been restricted from the dance because of what happened to Roger Greenfoot last night."

"Oh, no!" April exclaimed, her dreams of the dance shattered. How could Roger do this to Todd? Why did he have to punish her, too?

Todd didn't show up for lunch and he was late for Music Appreciation. When he finally arrived, he chose a seat by the door on the opposite side of the room from April. She was sure he was going to make a quick getaway again after class, but he surprised her and waited outside the door.

He looked at the ground, kicking at the dirt. "Did you hear what happened?"

"Jon told me. I'm so sorry," April said softly.

Todd forced a smile. "Well, you'll have a good time, anyway."

"No, I won't. I was looking forward to dancing with you." She clenched her fists. "It's just not fair!"

"No, it's not," he agreed. "But they're setting an example. Boy, I can't believe how much old Rog got away with last year when *he* was a camper! I'll bet he suggested the dance restriction."

"I may not go either," April said.

Todd shook his head. "Please go. You shouldn't miss your first camp dance."

"Okay, I guess," she whispered sadly, wondering why she agreed.

"I've got to go," Todd said. "If I'm late for rest hour, it'll give Rog another excuse to get mad."

That evening April stood in her stockinged feet near the door of the dining hall where the dance was being held. She had left her sneakers in the pile outside, rolled up her jeans, and pulled her hair back into a high ponytail to look like a girl from the fifties. Although April looked festive, she still wished she hadn't promised Todd she'd come without him.

"Wrap your mittens around your kittens, and let's rock and roll!" Greg shouted in an imitation of a fifties-style disc jockey. He switched on the tape, and the beat of the music filled the large room. Boys and girls paired up and began to dance while April watched glumly. Even Roger was dancing up a storm, she noticed, and hoped somebody would step on his big green foot.

After an hour or so, the noise began to bother her. Though she'd danced with many of the guys, April's thoughts were only of Todd in his cabin. She wondered what he was doing. Was he lying on his bunk, listening to the music? Was he thinking about her, wishing they were together?

"HELLO!" Karen waved her hand in front of April's face, bringing her back to reality.

She smiled and shook her head. "Sorry— I just don't feel very 'up' tonight. I think I'll go outside for a while. See you later." April pushed her way through the dancers and slipped outside, glad no one had stopped her.

She found her sneakers in the pile of shoes and put them on. Then, dropping onto a bench, she tipped her head back, gazing up at the beautiful sky. The stars twinkled like crystal droplets against the inky background, and April quickly found the Big Dipper. Somehow she thought of it as belonging exclusively to her and Todd. Maybe he was looking at it right now, too. . . .

At first she thought she imagined the voice. But then she heard it again, very softly. "April, over here!" She looked around but saw nothing. Then, as her eyes adjusted to the darkness beyond the porch, she saw a shadowy outline next to a big pine tree not far away. Todd! She checked to see that no one was watching, then ran to meet him.

"What are you doing here?" she whispered in delighted surprise.

"I wanted to dance with you," Todd said, reaching for her hand. The music had changed to a slow tune, and it drifted up the hill to where they stood.

April shivered as he drew her into his arms. Her heart was pounding so hard that she thought Todd would feel it through his cable-knit sweater.

"Your hair smells good—like wildflowers," Todd whispered as they swayed together in rhythm with the music. April shut her eyes, savoring the closeness. When the song ended, he held her for a long moment before

72

he released her. "Let's find a piano," he said, taking her hand. "There's one in the rec hall."

As they walked along the dark path, April wondered why Todd had suddenly decided to play the piano, but she remained silent, not wanting to break the magic between them.

Todd opened the screen door and eased it shut. He sat down at the piano and April slid in close next to him.

"There's this song I wrote—I want to play it for you." He ran his fingers over the keys. He began to sing very softly in a clear tenor voice:

"Fly away with me—for a while,
Take my hand, make a stand,
  Share my love.

We'll fly over all the earth,
Swirling high, you and I—
  Love's rebirth.

Come to my heart that's open wide,
Create a dream, be a team,
  Side by side.

I know our love is here to stay—
Together we, you and me,
  We'll fly away."

"It's beautiful," April whispered when he finished. She was so moved by the song that she could hardly speak.

Todd turned to her. "I was wondering if maybe you'd like to learn it and sing it with me for Slumber Music next week."

April gasped. "Oh, yes! I mean—I don't know if I could. I might mess it up."

"I'll teach you. We'll have plenty of time to practice."

The thought of practicing with Todd and *only* with Todd made up her mind. "Okay, I'll try," she said.

"It's a deal then!" He moved closer to her. Sliding his arm around her waist, he brushed her lips with his in a tender kiss, "To seal the bargain," he told her.

April felt giddy. Even if the kiss meant only a bargain sealed to Todd, it meant everything to her. She tried to memorize the touch of his lips so she would be able to relive it over and over again.

"We'd better go—I hear voices and that means the dance must be over."

As they started toward the door, April saw two people peering through the screen— Karen and Jon.

Karen grinned at her. "We've been looking all over for you."

"I wasn't going to hang out in the cabin alone, so I decided to find some company!" Jon said to Todd with a large grin.

"Well, buddy, it's almost lights-out, and

you and I better not be missing when Rog comes in," Todd said, urging them up the path.

As they hurried along, April noticed that Karen and Jon held hands.

After the boys raced off through the woods toward their cabin, April and Karen tiptoed into Cabin One. Most of the others were already in their sleeping bags, so the two girls took their toothbrushes and went into the bathroom where they could talk without disturbing anyone.

"So what were you and Todd up to, snuggling on that piano bench?" Karen asked, her eyes dancing.

"He wanted to sing me a song he had written. And, Karen, I'm so excited! He asked me to sing it with him for Slumber Music next week!"

Karen gave her a big hug. "That's fantastic!"

"Hey, what's going on with you and Jon?" April asked. "When did you two get so chummy?"

"If you hadn't been so wrapped up in Todd, you would have noticed that we spent a lot of time together at Lake Arrowhead," Karen said with a smirk.

April began brushing her teeth. "I thought you were just being friendly," she said.

"Well, we were, and then we got a lot friendlier!"

They finished in the bathroom, then rushed

back to the sleeping porch, slipping into their bunks just as the French horn finished the last note of taps.

Karen leaned down and whispered, "Sweet dreams."

"Guaranteed!" April whispered back.

Chapter Eight

On Monday morning, April clenched and unclenched her sweaty hands and kept shifting her position in the metal folding chair. Why had she ever decided to audition for a solo in Girls' Chorus? She must have been out of her mind! She wished her turn would come so she could get it over with before she tied herself in nervous knots. April had no idea she would have to try out in front of everyone, or else she would never have signed up.

Karen leaned over and whispered, "Connie's next."

Now alert, April prepared to listen to each note. She saw Connie take a deep breath before she began to sing. Could Connie also be nervous? If she was, it certainly didn't show in her voice. April turned to Karen. "She's awfully good."

"So are you," Karen responded.

As Connie returned to her seat on a wave of applause, her eyes met April's and she flashed a triumphant smile.

"April Sullivan," Mrs. Harper announced.

April sat glued to her chair. She just couldn't go up there! She'd make a fool of herself. She'd have to get out of it somehow.

"April?" Mrs. Harper asked.

Karen nudged her. "Go for it!"

April managed to stand up and walk slowly to the front. Her knees felt like jelly. What if they buckled under while she sang? What if she croaked like a frog when she opened her mouth? She swallowed a few times, crossed her fingers, and nodded to the accompanist to begin playing "The Rose." After a few shaky notes, April's fear subsided. She forgot everything except the song, which was so familiar that it almost seemed to sing itself.

When it was over she practically collapsed into her chair. "You were great!" Karen whispered as the applause ended and the next girl started to sing. From across the room, Sandy held her thumb up. But April shook her head. Hadn't they heard how her voice had quivered at first, or noticed how scared she'd been? She was sure that anyone who got so nervous would never be given a solo. Looking over at Connie, who sat proudly, April decided that she'd probably get one of the solos. Connie didn't seem afraid of anything.

April closed her eyes, letting the rest of the tryouts fade into the background. She thought about Saturday night and how wonderful the time had been with Todd.

It had been a little disappointing not to see more of him yesterday, but Sunday's routine was slightly different from the weekday one and Todd had gone directly from Music Appreciation class to lunch with Jon and some other friends. April hadn't had a chance to be with him until free time, and then he played the piano while she sang along with the group of kids that hung around him.

"Okay, girls, that's it. I'll let you know my decision in a couple of days," Mrs. Harper said. Everyone got up and headed for the doors.

Sandy joined April and Karen. "Let's go to lunch—I'm starving!"

"You're *always* starving," Karen teased.

"You go ahead," April said. "I want to talk to Mrs. Harper for a minute."

"Catch up when you're through," Karen called.

"Can I help you with something, April?" Mrs. Harper asked, removing her glasses and rubbing the bridge of her nose.

"I noticed the other day that you had a

songbook with guitar chords," April said. "I was wondering if I could borrow it for this afternoon."

"Oh, you play the guitar?" Mrs. Harper rummaged in her big canvas bag and finally pulled out a book. "Here it is. And take your time. I'm not using it at all this session."

April glanced down at the list of songs. "Thanks a lot! I really appreciate it. I didn't bring any guitar music with me." She started to hurry after her friends, but the teacher's voice stopped her.

"April?" She turned to see Mrs. Harper smiling at her. "Nice job today."

"Thank you!" April couldn't believe her ears. Had she really done well? "I guess you could tell I felt a little nervous."

"So did everyone else. Now go to lunch or you'll be late."

April felt like skipping to the dining hall. She hadn't been terrible! A little scared—no, a *lot* scared, but Mrs. Harper didn't seem to care. She caught up with Karen and Sandy a moment later, and was so excited she could hardly breathe.

"What were you doing?" Sandy asked.

"Well, I borrowed a book." April hesitated and then added, "She said she liked my tryout!"

"April, that's great!" they chorused. "Now let's eat!"

During free time, April sat under a cedar tree, looking through the guitar book. She'd found many of her old favorites and a few new songs she wanted to learn. Taking a small black notebook out of her guitar case, she began copying the chords. Then, she found a familiar camp song, and experimented with the chords, adding some of her own. She smiled and decided she'd have to play it for Karen and Sandy. In the distance, she heard voices from the pool area and the sound of a piano drifting from the Choir Bowl. Looking up, she saw Jackie coming toward her. "I didn't know you played the guitar," Jackie said as she plopped down on the grass next to April.

"I didn't bring any music, so I borrowed this book from Mrs. Harper."

"Great! You'll have to play for campfire some night."

Suddenly April noticed that Jackie was wearing a name tag. This was unusual because she hadn't ever noticed it before *and* because the name on the tag wasn't even Jackie's.

"What's with Greg's name tag?" she asked, puzzled.

"Camp custom. It shows you're taken," Jackie explained. "You just trade tags."

April tried to remember if she'd ever seen Todd wearing his name tag. "That's neat. I wish . . ."

"Maybe Todd will want to trade," Jackie said, grinning.

"Oh, no!" April groaned. "Is it that obvious?"

Jackie laughed. "To me, it is. Well, I've got to run. See you later." She jumped up and headed toward the pool.

Stretching, April got to her feet and packed up her guitar. On the way back to her cabin, she passed three girls from Cabin Two. She smiled and said, "Hello," but they looked away. April stared after them, wondering what was bothering them, then shrugged and continued on her way.

She heard Karen and Sandy talking as she approached the screen door to the sleeping porch. "Of course it's not true!" Karen said emphatically.

Sandy sounded doubtful. "Well, she *did* stay after class, and she told us Mrs. Harper said she'd done a good job."

"I'm positive she wouldn't do a thing like that!" Karen snapped. "It's just one of Connie's nasty tricks."

"Yeah, I guess you're right. April's not the type . . ."

April stepped onto the porch. "I'm not what type?"

Embarrassed, Sandy looked away.

"Connie's making trouble," Karen said. "She's spread the word that you stayed after Girls' Chorus to score points with Mrs. Harper so she'd give you a solo."

"That's not true! I only borrowed a book!" April protested angrily.

"We believe you. I'm sorry I even questioned it for a second. But the rumor's already spread around camp." Sandy said.

"We'll take care of it, don't worry," Karen assured April grimly. "We'll start at supper."

April threw herself down on her bunk, burying her face in the pillow. "I can't face everyone if they think Connie's telling the truth! I'll skip supper."

"No, you won't!" Karen snatched the pillow away. "If you don't show up, everyone will believe Connie."

A tear trickled down April's cheek and she wiped it away. "Why does she hate me so much?"

"It's got to be Todd," Sandy said, consoling April. "She wants him and you've got him. She's just jealous."

"The reason doesn't matter. She's being sneaky and mean." Karen bent down by April's bunk. "C'mon, April, I told you we'll take care of it."

April appreciated her friends' support. But could Karen and Sandy convince the whole camp that Connie was lying? She got up from her bunk, and Karen shoved her out the cabin door. "Let's go. We don't want to be late and make a grand entrance."

Heads turned toward them as the three entered the dining hall. April felt hostile eyes burning her back as she got her food and followed her friends to a table where several campers were sitting. When they sat down, two of the girls picked up their plates and moved to another table.

April started to get up and leave, too, but Karen pulled her back down. "Cool it!" she cried. "You're acting guilty!"

"How can I act normal when everyone looks like they're ready to murder me?" April almost *felt* guilty, as if she were on trial and the jury had reached a verdict without hearing her defense. Oh, why had she ever stayed behind to borrow that darned book?

Karen got up from the bench. "I'll be back in a little while." She began going from table to table, talking to the campers.

April couldn't eat. She held her breath when Todd came into the dining room. He filled his plate and started in her direction. But when Jon waved him over to his table, he smiled ruefully at April as he walked toward Jon's table. At least he wasn't acting as though April were a condemned criminal.

Supper seemed to last forever. Karen and Sandy took turns talking to the other kids, and April was very grateful to her two friends, though she still felt humiliated. It would have been horrible to face this alone. Remembering her mom's "friends lecture," she realized how right she was.

Suddenly a shrill bell began ringing somewhere outside.

Conversation stopped for a moment. Then the campers began laughing and talking louder than ever. Roger jumped up and raced for the door, shouting angrily, "It's Mr. Box!" Many of the kids rushed out after him.

"Mr. Box strikes again!" someone yelled from the back.

"C'mon, April!" Sandy said. "We'll introduce you to Mr. Box!"

Mystified, April followed Sandy and joined the group gathered around the tall pine tree in front of the dining hall. Looking up, she saw a metal box with a smiley face on it tied to one of the lower limbs. The shrill ringing seemed to be coming from the box.

"Mr. Box makes a lot of appearances each year," Karen yelled over the voices of the kids and the noise of the bell. "He keeps showing up in different spots."

April raised her voice, too. "That's bizarre. Who does it?"

"No one knows," Sandy shouted. "I think Todd and Jon are in on it this time. Roger thinks so, too, but he can't prove it." She giggled. "Hey, look at Rog now!"

April watched as Roger climbed up the trunk of the tree and began banging at the box with a hammer. Everyone else was whooping and cheering him on, and again April felt like an outsider. Connie's nasty rumor had spoiled everything. Thanks to Connie, April was afraid things would never be the same.

Chapter Nine

April thought evening choir rehearsal would never end. As she sang, she stared into space and couldn't help thinking that maybe she never really had fit in at camp.

When rehearsal finally finished, April found herself surrounded by all the girls from Cabin One's sleeping porch. They assured her that they didn't believe the rumor, and volunteered to help Karen and Sandy spread the word to the rest of camp about the dirty trick Connie had played.

"Rumor-busters, unite!" Sandy cried, and everyone laughed.

"Oh, here comes Jon!" Karen's eyes lit up as she and April separated from the rest of the group.

Jon walked over to April and patted her on the head. "Congratulations! I hear you and Mrs. Harper are great friends," he said before ducking.

"Leave her alone!" Karen flew at him, pounding him with both fists.

April didn't know whether to be mad or to laugh, so she joined Karen in punching him.

"Help!" Jon yelled, holding up his arms in front of his face to ward off the blows. "Just kidding! I take it all back."

"Hey, what are you doing to my buddy?" Todd called as he came over to them. He grabbed April around the waist and pulled her away from Jon, holding her close.

April stopped struggling and leaned back against him. Every time he came near, her skin tingled and her pulse began beating a mile a minute.

"Serves you right, you troublemaker!" Karen got in one last punch before she quit, and smiled sweetly up at Jon.

"So what was that all about?" Todd asked.

April glanced apprehensively at him. Had he heard the ugly rumor? Could he possibly believe it? If he even suspected she could do such a thing, she would die right there on the spot.

"Connie spread all that dirt about April trying to talk Mrs. Harper into giving her a solo," Karen told him.

Todd raised his eyebrows. "Connie? Why would she do that?"

"She's jealous of April," Sandy said.

"She's afraid April will get a solo instead of her," Karen explained. She smiled at April. "Connie's good, all right, but not the best."

"I can't believe Connie would do that," Todd said. "I mean, I've known her so long . . ."

April felt awful. Todd was actually defending Connie after she'd done such an awful thing!

"Wake up, Todd!" Karen sounded exasperated. "You don't know what she's really like."

"Well, whoever did it, it was a dirty trick," he said. "Now I want to talk to April." He took her hand and led her away from the others.

Out of the corner of her eye, April saw Jon and Karen walking toward the rec hall and almost wished she were going with them. *If Todd wants to believe Connie,* she thought, *then I don't know if I care about him anymore.* Well, that wasn't exactly true, but she felt unhappy and hurt.

Todd pointed to a nearby bench. "Let's sit down a minute."

April sat and stared down at her tennis shoes, keeping a distance between herself and Todd.

"April, you have to know that I don't believe any of that stuff," he said. "C'mon, cheer up."

When she didn't respond, he added, "I was wondering if we could practice our song tomorrow. You're still going to do Slumber Music with me, aren't you?"

His question made April feel better. "Sure. Tomorrow will be fine."

"You don't sound very enthusiastic."

"It's just that it's been such a horrible day . . ." She glanced up and saw Todd looking at her with so much concern that it melted her heart and she smiled. "I'm sorry for being so moody. I'd love to work on the song with you."

Now Todd smiled, too. "Great! Let's work together tomorrow during free time, okay?"

April nodded. "Okay."

The next day after Music Theory and rehearsals, Todd and April went back to the rec hall. "I didn't think you'd want to practice in the Choir Bowl with everyone hanging around," he explained as they entered the building.

April was grateful to him for understanding how she felt about rehearsing in front of a crowd. As they sat side by side on the piano bench, she noticed that Todd wasn't wearing his name tag, and she caught her breath, remembering what Jackie had said about exchanging badges. Had he given it to someone else?

"Where's your name tag?" she asked casually, almost afraid to hear his answer. But she had to know.

"Oh, I never wear it after the first day of

camp." He grinned at her. "Why? Do you keep forgetting who I am?"

"Well, it's so hard to keep track of everybody," she teased, and giggled when he punched her lightly on the arm. At least he hadn't given it to Connie or some other girl!

Todd started to play the song. "I'll sing it through first," he said. "I thought I'd do the first verse as a solo, and then I'll teach you the harmony."

April watched his face while she listened to his rich tenor voice, and thought, *If only those words had been written for me. I'd love to fly away with him!*

When Todd finished singing, April applauded softly. "That's great. I really don't think you need me. I told you—I'll probably just mess it up."

"Why do you always put yourself down?" he asked, looking at her seriously.

April avoided his eyes. "I don't know—I guess it's because everybody is so talented here. All of a sudden I don't seem to be very good."

"April, you have a terrific voice." He reached out and took her hand in both of his. "I could have asked anyone to sing this with me, but I wanted *you* because I knew our voices would blend perfectly."

His words restored her faith in herself. Somehow she'd find the confidence to do a fantastic job, both for herself and for Todd.

After about an hour, she had perfected the

harmony and was becoming familiar with the lyrics.

Todd struck a final chord and stretched his arms overhead. "That's enough for today. Why don't you copy down the words so you can memorize them? It'll be pretty dark out there, and all we'll have is the light on the piano."

Singing in the dark with Todd sounded wonderful to April. As she wrote down the lyrics of the song, she was sure she'd have no trouble learning them by heart.

When she had finished, Todd gave her a quick hug. "C'mon—let's go. My stomach says it's almost suppertime."

April headed for her cabin, feeling warm and happy inside. Todd seemed pleased with the progress they'd made at rehearsal. Most important, he seemed pleased with *her*. And by now, everyone at camp knew that Connie had started the nasty rumor yesterday. It was amazing how things could change in just twenty-four hours!

Then suddenly Connie appeared on the pathway, coming toward her. Instead of flinching, April quickened her step. Nothing was going to drag her down today. She had enough confidence from this afternoon to tackle even Connie.

When Connie saw April, she hesitated. Then, narrowing her eyes, she kept on walking until the two girls were face-to-face.

April took a deep breath. "Connie, I want to talk to you."

"I don't have anything to say to a brown-noser," Connie sneered.

"What made you spread that rumor about me? You don't really believe it, do you?" April questioned.

"Why shouldn't I believe it?" Connie lifted her chin defiantly. "You *did* stay after tryouts to have a chummy little private talk."

"I borrowed her songbook, that's all."

"Yeah, right! And you didn't say a single word about the auditions, I guess."

Connie started to walk on, but April blocked her way. "You know you did it on purpose to get me into trouble. What's wrong? Are you jealous?" April retorted.

"Why should I be jealous of you?" Connie sneered. "You think you're really something, don't you? You come to Bear Mountain for the first time and think you can just take over, and have everything your own way. Well, don't think you're going to get Todd and a solo, too!"

She pushed her way around April and ran toward the boys' side of camp.

Amazed at Connie's words, April stood staring after her. How could anyone be so wrong? If Connie only knew how scared she'd been about coming to camp, and how concerned she'd been about what everybody thought of her.

Well, April wasn't scared now. She had so much to look forward to . . . Slumber Music with Todd . . . being with Karen and Sandy . . . the final concert. Right now, she felt on top of the world.

Chapter Ten

The next day's Slumber Music rehearsal started out seriously. April and Todd sang the song four times, stopping when they hit a rough spot, or when the harmony didn't sound quite right to Todd's professional ear. Finally they made it all the way through on the fifth try.

"We're ready!" Todd announced, picking up an empty juice can and using it for a microphone. He stepped up onto the piano bench. "And now ladies and gentlemen, we bring you the new singing stars that are holding audiences spellbound with their brilliant performance! Discovered at Bear Mountain Music Camp, April Sullivan and Todd Barrett have just been nominated 'Talent Discovery of the Year!' "

"Stop it!" April giggled. "Everybody will hear you!"

"How can we be discovered if no one hears us?" Todd jumped down and grabbed April's hand. "Let's go find someone to tell us how good we are."

"We can't do that!" April's horrified look made Todd laugh.

Just as Todd began pulling her toward the door, Jon walked in the rec hall. "Doesn't look much like practice to me."

"We are soooo good," Todd drawled. "So good that we don't need to practice anymore."

April clapped a hand over his mouth. "We're not *that* good," she said. "We still need to work on it. Todd's just tired of practicing."

Jon turned to Todd. "So if you're finished practicing for today, are you ready for our next project?"

"Project?" April echoed, removing her hand from over Todd's mouth.

"Just something we're working on," Jon explained.

Todd put his arm around April's shoulders. "We can tell her. She won't give us away."

Bewildered, April looked from Todd to Jon. "What's going on this time?"

Jon whispered in her ear. "Mr. Box will soon strike again—or *ring* again."

April giggled. "I *knew* it! I knew all that stuff you bought in Arrowhead wasn't just to paint Roger's feet!"

"We have to find a place for him," Todd remarked as he turned to April. "Want to come?"

April saw Jon's frown and said, "Thanks, but I think I'll go soak up some rays instead."

That night, April lay on her bunk, listening to Karen and Sandy sing their duet for Slumber Music. She smiled, thinking about tomorrow when she'd be singing with Todd, and wondered if they would sound as good as today. Todd seemed to think they were terrific, but April felt her voice sounded untrained compared to his. Still, he kept encouraging her, and that made her feel good.

After supper the following evening, April sat on the porch outside the dining hall, watching the sunset's rosy clouds squeeze the orange sun into a fat jack-o'-lantern. She didn't feel like socializing tonight. Her stomach was queasy, but she knew it was just nerves. Todd was so cool about the whole thing. He couldn't understand how shaky she felt. But she was excited, too. How could she be so scared and excited at the same time?

The sun slowly sank behind the mountains, silhouetting them against a red glow. In less than an hour it would be dark. She went over the lyrics to the song and hummed the music under her breath. Then she walked toward her cabin where she intended to rest until it was time to sing.

Karen found her there a while later, when she and Sandy came into the cabin. "There you are," she said. "I figured you'd hidden yourself somewhere."

Sandy took April's hand and squeezed it. "It's going to be fine. Quit worrying."

"Jackie's looking for you, too," Karen added. "She wanted to make sure you were ready."

"Ready as I'll ever be." April got up and threw on her soft teal-green sweater, and brushed her hair. Even though it would be dark, she wanted to look her best for her moonlight rendezvous with Todd.

When the other girls started filtering back into the cabin and getting ready for bed, April's anticipation increased. It was almost time to head for the Choir Bowl where Todd would meet her.

"Did you find April?" she heard Jackie's voice call out.

"I'm in here!" April called back.

Karen and Sandy both gave her a hug. "Good luck!"

"I'll need it," she murmured as she left the sleeping porch.

To her surprise, Jackie was waiting for her. "I have to go with you," Jackie said. "Camp rules—a girl and a guy can't go out together after dark without a chaperon."

April's spirits dropped. Her idea of a romantic evening definitely *didn't* include Jackie. In her dreams, it had been just the two of them, alone by the piano. She sighed as she turned on her flashlight and started along the path to the Choir Bowl with Jackie at her side.

"I'll wait up here," Jackie said when they saw Todd's flashlight bobbing toward them.

"Scared?" Todd asked, coming up to April.

"How'd you guess?"

Together they entered the Choir Bowl and walked to the piano. April could barely see Jackie taking a seat high up in the Bowl. The night was very dark because the moon was hidden behind thick clouds. Todd took April's hand and squeezed it reassuringly before he sat down and turned on the small lamp over the music. A cool breeze ruffled her hair, and April was glad she'd worn a warm sweater. In spite of the chill, her hands felt damp and sticky.

Please don't let me blow it, she prayed. What if she opened her mouth and nothing came out? What would Todd do if she ruined their duet? She wanted to sing perfectly for him—but could she?

Todd looked up at her and smiled. "Ready?"

April nodded. She felt her knees tremble as she sat next to him on the bench. Todd began to play the introduction. *How different it sounds here in the dark,* April thought—moody and almost mysterious. When his voice sang the first lines, she gripped the piano bench to steady herself. He finished the verse and nodded for her to join him.

Once April was actually singing, her shaking stopped. She lost herself in the music, looking at Todd as she sang. Their voices blended perfectly, and April knew they had never sounded better. When the song ended, the last note lingered with the tenderness of a caress, and they sat silently side by side. April hardly dared breathe, afraid to destroy the beauty of the moment. At last Todd reached up to turn out the piano light, and April stood up.

"April," Todd whispered. He too had gotten up and now stood very close to her in the dark. The breeze whispered through the leaves of the trees, and taps was the only sound in the still night. Todd reached out and gently pulled her to him. She slipped into his arms, resting her head on his chest.

The clouds parted and moonlight flooded the Choir Bowl, giving the night a magical quality. *Will I wake up and find it's really a dream?* April thought. *It's so like what I've dreamed before, how can it possibly be true?*

Todd tilted her chin up, and gazed into her eyes. He traced one finger along her cheek, sending tingles through her. April shivered and he held her more tightly. Her pulse raced as he bent down and lightly kissed her lips.

"Oh, Todd . . ." she whispered as if saying his name would make it more real. His only answer was to kiss her again, more deeply this time. Then he held her in his arms for a long, enchanted moment.

"We've got to go," Todd whispered.

"I know."

He released her slowly and kissed her cheek. " 'Night, April. See you tomorrow."

As she turned to leave the Choir Bowl, she remembered Jackie. Had she been watching? April blushed at the thought.

But when Jackie joined her a few minutes later, all she said was, "It sounded terrific. Good job!"

"Thanks," April murmured, and they walked along in silence. April wanted to savor those moments with Todd, and Jackie seemed to understand.

When they slipped into the cabin, all was quiet. Jackie patted her shoulder and whispered goodnight.

The moonlight flooded the porch and revealed Karen propped on her elbow. April didn't really want to talk, but she knew Karen was waiting to hear all about it. *Just one more second*, April thought, closing her eyes and remembering Todd's kisses. Only ten minutes ago she'd been in his arms! She hugged herself and tiptoed to Karen's bunk.

"You were both wonderful," Karen whispered. "I had tears in my eyes." She leaned over the bunk. "Anything interesting happen?"

"It was really special," April said softly.

"Come on, April! Are you going to keep me in suspense all night? Did he kiss you?"

Suddenly April just had to share her excitement with her friend. "Yes, he did. Oh, Karen, it was so wonderful!"

"I knew it! I knew he would!" Karen squealed and then clamped her hand over her mouth.

April finished changing and crawled into her sleeping bag. "This is the best night of my life," she sighed.

"I'll bet," Karen said. "Todd's a great guy. You're really lucky."

April smiled. "I know."

Chapter Eleven

Several days later, Todd and Jon didn't show up for breakfast, and the dining hall seemed less crowded than usual. "Who's missing besides Todd and Jon?" April asked Karen.

"Looks like their whole cabin disappeared," Karen said. As Sandy arrived with her tray, Karen asked, "Where are all the guys?"

"Roger's giving them a lecture."

Amazed at Sandy's ability to find out everything that happened at camp, even in the boys' cabin, April shook her head.

"Guess we slept through all the excitement," Sandy added.

"What excitement? Tell us!" Karen urged.

Sandy sat down between them. "Well, when

good old Rog got into his bunk late last night, Mr. Box went off! It took him about ten minutes to get the thing unwired. He was furious."

"How do you know all this?" April asked.

"My own special news service." She giggled. "Anyway, that's why Rog is reading them the riot act."

"Does Roger know who did it?" April asked anxiously.

Sandy shook her head. "No—I think they all helped."

April relaxed a little. She knew that Todd and Jon had been in on it, and she didn't want them to get in trouble again.

April didn't see Todd until Music Appreciation. After class, they met outside. "We really got to Rog this time," Todd told her gleefully as they headed for chorus practice. They jogged together to April's rehearsal hall. Then he kissed her on the cheek and left for Boys' Chorus.

When rehearsal was over, April walked back to the cabin to wash up for lunch. Karen followed and handed April a postcard and a letter. "Mail call!" she announced.

The postcard was from Janie, saying how great Italy was. April thought for a second how much had happened this summer without Janie even knowing a thing! She couldn't wait to share her exciting news with her best friend. She recognized her own familiar address on the envelope of the letter. Ripping it open, she flopped down on her bunk to read all the news from home. When she reached the last part of the letter, April gasped.

We sure do miss you, honey, but now that camp is almost over, we'll be seeing you soon.

Love,
Mom

The words leapt off the page: ". . . CAMP IS ALMOST OVER . . ." It hardly seemed possible! With only one week left, April realized that she might never see Todd again! For the first time in ages, she thought about the girl he had phoned, and her heart sank.

"April!" Karen broke into her thoughts. "This isn't rest hour. C'mon!"

"I'm just realizing how little time we have left at camp." April sighed.

"Yeah. Bummer, isn't it?"

April knew Karen hated to leave Jon. Even with all the clowning the two of them did, April knew they cared for each other a lot.

April and Karen didn't say much as they headed for the dining hall, and neither of them felt very hungry.

After lunch April wandered over to the Choir Bowl ahead of the others for full choir rehearsal. She had learned to love the music, even with all the Latin words. It was funny, considering how difficult and intimidating it had all seemed at first.

As she took her music from the rack, she heard a voice behind her.

April turned around and found Todd smiling at her.

"Hey, early bird, what's the rush?" he asked.

April thought how nice he looked today. His beige T-shirt almost matched his sandy hair and contrasted with his dark brown shorts. Then she noticed that he had pinned his name tag on the pocket of his shirt. She wondered why he'd bothered to put it on at this late date. Many of the campers had already traded name tags—could Todd possibly want to exchange tags with her?

Paul Browning rapped his stick on the music stand to get everyone's attention, and April joined Sandy in the alto section.

"Today's the big day," Mrs. Harper announced, smiling at the campers. "I have decided on the girls' soloists for our final concert."

An excited squeal came from behind April and everyone laughed. Mrs. Harper laughed, too. "Our first soloist is a veteran camper, a girl with a beautiful voice, and I think everyone will agree she'll do a fine job. Take a bow, Connie Saturo!"

As Connie stood up and beamed triumphantly, April joined halfheartedly in the applause. When the clapping subsided, Mrs. Harper continued, "Connie will be doing the solo in the Hungarian folk medley. And our second soloist"—April held her breath—"is a newcomer . . . April Sullivan!"

April was stunned. She'd actually won a solo! "I can't believe it!" she gasped.

"Stand up, dummy," Sandy teased, giving her a push. As everyone applauded, April turned to see Karen giving her a thumbs-up from the soprano section, and Todd grinning at her. "Congratulations!" he mouthed.

Sandy pounded her on the back when she sat down again. "I knew you could do it!"

"I'm so excited!" April cried.

She listened in delight as Mrs. Harper announced that "The Rose" would be her song.

"Me! It's really me!" she whispered to herself. "And I know I can do it. I'm not scared anymore!"

Later that afternoon, during free time, April searched for Todd, eager to share her excitement. She'd been to the Choir Bowl, hoping to find him at the piano, but he wasn't there. Where could he be? She hadn't seen him since rehearsal.

She wandered up to the volleyball court. Several people were playing, but not Todd.

Retracing her steps, she crossed the bridge

above the campfire site and saw Jon sitting on one of the logs around the fire pit. Maybe he'd seen Todd. She climbed down the wide steps cut out of the steep bank and hurried over to where he sat.

Jon looked up and grinned. "What's up?"

April sat down beside him. "Do you know where Todd is?" she asked, concerned.

"I haven't seen him since rehearsal. Hey, congrats on your solo."

"Thanks!" April smiled.

"You might find Todd checking out the mail. He said something about expecting a letter," Jon added.

"Okay. See you at campfire tonight!"

April ran up the steps and headed for the main building. She didn't find Todd, but there was a pile of letters on the mail table.

Since Todd's cabin's pile just happened to be on top, April sifted through the mound. A square, pink envelope caught her eye. Seeing Todd's name on it, she peered at it. *It must be from a girl*, she thought, noticing the delicate handwriting. On impulse she picked it up. The envelope reeked of flowery perfume, and the name above the return address was Nancy Adams. *Nancy*—the same girl Todd had called. April dropped the envelope back on the table. It had to be from his girlfriend back home. All summer she had tried to forget that there was someone else in Todd's life, but she couldn't do it anymore. Soon he'd be going back to Nancy, and April would have only a bittersweet memory of a brief summer romance.

Tears burned her eyes as she walked away. She didn't want to find Todd now. Oh, why did love hurt so much?

Chapter Twelve

The sun had already set that evening as April carried her guitar down the steps to the campfire circle. Campers were seated on the logs that surrounded the blaze, laughing and talking. Across from her, April spotted Jackie with Greg and some other counselors who would lead the singing. She hesitated. Jackie had asked her to play at campfire many times, but this was the first time she had decided to give it a try. At least it might help her to forget about Todd and Nancy.

"Hey, April!" Jackie called. "Glad you finally decided to play for us."

"If I waited any longer, camp would be over," April replied, trying to sound more cheerful than she felt. Though Todd waved to her and pointed at a space next to him, she pretended not to see him, and joined Jackie instead.

Playing while the campers sang was easier than April had anticipated. She knew most of the songs, and when they sang one she didn't know, she either improvised or tapped out the rhythm on the side of her guitar. *I really feel like I belong here now*, she thought sadly. *If only I belonged with Todd . . .*

As the blazing fire subsided to glowing embers, April looked up and saw Todd staring at her with a puzzled expression. She shivered and quickly turned back to her guitar. Would she ever be able to forget him? April sighed. She'd just have to, that's all.

The warning bell rang, signaling the end of campfire. April saw Karen and Sandy talking to Jon and Todd, then watched as Todd waved to someone she couldn't see. Not wanting to talk to the others, April trudged slowly up the steps. She paused on the wooden bridge, lost in her own thoughts. After a while she gazed across the camp and saw a light in one of the phone booths. Even from this distance, she recognized Todd inside. She swallowed hard to get rid of the lump in her throat. He must be calling Nancy now. It would only be natural to call your girlfriend when you'd just gotten a letter from her. Feeling miserable and lonely, April walked slowly back to Cabin One.

April didn't sleep much that night, but she did a lot of thinking. She decided that she had to stop dreaming and face the fact that though she'd fallen head over heels in love with Todd, he was obviously one of those guys who liked to play the field. From now until the end of camp, she'd play it totally cool and not show Todd how much she really cared.

April arrived at the dining hall for supper the following evening before Karen or Sandy, so she helped herself to the beef stew and found an empty table to save some places. As she sat down, she heard Todd's voice behind her.

"Any room for me?" he asked, resting his tray on her head.

April was surprised to see him, since he had seemed to be avoiding her all day. "Sure—be my guest," she said. He set his tray down and sat next to her.

"You look good in pink, April."

April felt her pulse quicken at his words. What was going on? He hadn't spoken to her since yesterday afternoon, and now he was flirting with her.

"I got a solo in Boys' Chorus for the final concert," Todd said casually.

"A solo? That's great! Why didn't they announce it?" April exclaimed, forgetting her vow to keep cool.

Todd laughed. "Hey, it's no big deal—only two bars." But April could tell he was pleased.

"I'm really happy for you," she said.

"What're you happy about?" Karen asked as she, Jon, and Sandy sat down at the table.

"Todd got a solo in the concert," April told her.

"Congratulations!" Karen cried.

"Is that why you've been hiding all day?" Sandy asked.

"I've been sort of busy." Todd glanced at Jon.

"You must have been," Karen added. "You didn't even play the piano during free time."

"Are you sure about that?" Jon grinned and started wolfing down his food.

Todd flashed him a warning look. "Cool it, Jon, okay?"

April wondered what they were talking about. If Todd had really been busy, maybe he *hadn't* been avoiding her. Not that it mattered, of course, she reminded herself sternly.

As soon as supper was over, Todd stood up. "Come outside," he whispered to April. "There's something I want to talk to you about."

Heart pounding, she followed him onto the porch. Was he going to tell her about the girl back home? If he did, she didn't know how she'd react.

Todd drew April aside, away from the other campers. "Do you want to help me tonight?"

April blinked. "With what?" she asked.

114

"I'm going to set off Mr. Box one last time." He looked around to make sure nobody could overhear him. "Want to give me a hand?"

After a moment's hesitation, April shrugged. "Why not? Should I dress all in black and wear a ski mask?"

Todd shook his head. "No. Just meet me at the bridge after rehearsal and I'll give you all the details."

"Doesn't Jon usually help you with stuff like this?" April asked.

"Yeah, but if Jon and I disappear and then the box goes off, Roger will be sure we did it. He'd never suspect you."

April knew Todd was right. Suddenly the idea of participating in Mr. Box's final appearance sounded like fun. Besides, she had to admit to herself that romance or no romance, she'd do anything, no matter how crazy, to spend more time with Todd.

After evening rehearsal, April hurried out of the Choir Bowl. She dashed to the cabin to grab a jacket, then ran down to the bridge. "Let's go!" Todd whispered as he came toward her from the other side.

"Where are we going?" April asked.

"You'll see." He took her hand and led the way down the steps, past the fire pit, and up a wooded slope on the other side.

There's no way I can stop caring about him, April thought. *But I can't let him know how I feel.*

"I'm going to anchor Mr. Box to the base

of this tree and set the timer," Todd said. "You find some rocks so we can hide it but it will still ring."

"Aye, aye, sir!" April saluted and set to work gathering rocks, which they piled around the contraption.

"Will anybody be able to hear it?" she asked. "We're pretty far away from the cabins."

Todd grinned. "Remember how loud it was that night at supper? They'll hear it, all right. Come on—let's get back before we're missed."

As they started down the slope, they heard the sound of someone crashing through the underbrush near the site of Mr. Box.

"Quick! Over here!" Todd pulled April, and they both crouched down behind a large tree. He put his arms tightly around her. April's heart was pounding, both from the fear of getting caught and from being so close to Todd. She was sure that her heartbeats could be heard all over camp.

The crunching, rustling noise came closer, then stopped abruptly. In the silence, April could hear an owl hooting in the distance, and a mosquito buzzing near her ear. Then she heard a soft padding sound behind her, just before a flashlight beam shone on her and Todd.

"What are you two doing out here?" Roger's nasal voice was unmistakable. "You know this is against the rules!"

April buried her face in Todd's shoulder and felt his arms tighten around her. "How'd you find us, Rog?" he asked. "Snooping around as usual?"

April couldn't see Roger's face, but she knew he must be furious. He motioned with the flashlight for them to get up. "We don't allow this kind of thing at camp," he said.

Oh, no! April thought, suddenly remembering what Jackie had said about couples always needing a chaperon. *He thinks we snuck off to be alone together!*

"It's not what you think . . ." she began, then broke off as Todd cut in.

"Jealous, Rog?" he joked.

"Get back where you belong, both of you!" Roger growled. "We'll see how much you're laughing when they take away your solo for the concert Saturday night, Barrett."

April caught her breath. Roger *couldn't* be that mean, could he? "Roger, it's not Todd's fault," she started to say, but once again Todd interrupted.

"Let's go, April," he said.

"Aren't you going to do anything?" April whispered to Todd as they walked away.

Todd shrugged. "What can I do? He's an exalted counselor—the jerk!—and I'm just a lowly camper."

When they reached the turnoff to Cabin One, April murmured, "Maybe he'll cool off by morning."

"Not good ol' Rog. But don't you worry."

Todd pulled her close. "I'm just sorry I dragged you into this," he whispered. Then he kissed her and jogged off toward the boys' cabins.

April touched her lips. They still tingled from his kiss, and she was filled with mixed emotions. On the one hand, she was thrilled that Todd had kissed her, though she wasn't sure what it meant to him. On the other hand, she was miserable at the thought that Todd would lose his solo. And what about her own solo? Would she be replaced? She'd hate that, but she couldn't let Todd take all the blame and all the punishment.

"Mr. Box!"

April awoke suddenly, leapt out of her bunk, and joined the shrieking, giggling girls who poured out of the cabin as the shrill bell shattered the silence of the night.

The whole camp can hear it, all right, she thought. *I wonder if Roger has figured out that's what Todd and I were really up to.*

The other girls were all talking at once, trying to guess who had set off Mr. Box this time.

"It couldn't be Todd and Jon," Karen declared, "because Jon spent the whole evening with me."

Sandy turned to April. "And you were with Todd, right?"

April nodded, relieved when no one asked

her any more questions. A moment later there was a loud crash, and the bell abruptly stopped ringing.

"Okay, gang. That's it for tonight!" Jackie herded the girls back inside. "We'll hear all about it in the morning."

April was afraid that she was right. She got back into her bunk and lay gazing into the dark. Surely Roger had guessed by now why she and Todd had been hiding in the woods. Maybe he'd change his mind about Todd's solo—after all, setting off Mr. Box wasn't against camp rules. In fact, it was a camp tradition.

April decided that first thing in the morning, she'd tell Jackie about her part in the stunt and ask her advice on what to do.

When April got to the dining hall, she saw Jackie talking to several other counselors. She hung around for a while until the other campers drifted in, then decided she might as well eat breakfast with her cabinmates and wait for a better time to approach Jackie.

Her opportunity came when she saw her counselor leaving the dining hall alone. April quickly dumped her tray and hurried after her, calling, "Jackie, wait! I need to talk to you!"

"What's up?" Jackie asked cheerfully. When she saw April's worried expression, she added, "Problems?"

119

April nodded. "Better believe it. Something happened last night . . ."

"It sure did," Jackie said, laughing. "I thought it was about time for Mr. Box to go off again, but I never imagined it would be at three o'clock in the morning. We're all trying to figure out who did it."

"I did," April confessed, to Jackie's astonishment. "Not all by myself. Todd wanted to do it and he asked me to help him, and now we're both in hot water."

"*Hot water* is right," Jackie said with a grin. "You'll both probably be washing dishes after supper tonight! KP is the only punishment for setting off Mr. Box. It's hardly anything to worry about."

"But that's not all," April told her. "Roger found us hiding in the woods. He didn't know what we were doing, but you can guess what he thought."

Jackie's eyes opened wider. "Hmm . . . that's a different story. What did Rog say?"

"He was furious, and he told Todd he was going to take his solo away," April said miserably.

Jackie stared at her. "You're kidding! Rog doesn't have the authority to do that."

"*He* thinks he does. Todd said he didn't care—it's only two bars—but I know it's important to him."

"He will probably try to persuade Mr. Collins that the two of you were fooling around out there."

"But we weren't!" April cried. "Honest, Jackie, all we were doing was rigging Mr. Box. Mr. Collins wouldn't take away Todd's solo for that, would he?" She hesitated, then added softly, "Or mine?"

"I honestly don't know, April. Rules are rules, and if Rog gets to Mr. Collins with his story before I can tell him what really happened—well, I just don't know." She looked at April assuringly. "I'll see what I can do. Meanwhile, hang in there, and try not to worry."

April watched as Jackie jogged down the path toward the camp director's office, a hollow feeling in the pit of her stomach.

Chapter Thirteen

After rehearsal later that morning, April sat with Todd at the piano in the Choir Bowl while the other campers straggled up to the dining hall to wait for the lunch bell. Neither of them had heard anything further about last night's adventure, and neither had much to say.

Suddenly April heard Jackie's voice calling her. She looked up and saw her counselor coming toward them. "Got a minute, April?" Jackie said. "I need to talk to you."

April swallowed hard. Was Jackie bringing bad news? Had they given her solo to somebody else?

Jackie turned to Todd. "Mind if I talk to April alone?"

Glancing anxiously from her to April, Todd

said, "No problem. See you at lunch, April, okay?"

April nodded. "What happened? Did you talk to Mr. Collins? Did *Roger* talk to Mr. Collins? What about our solos?" she asked Jackie nervously.

"Well, to begin with the *good* news," Jackie said, sitting next to April on the piano bench. "I got to Mr. C. before Rog did and explained the whole thing. There's no problem with your solo . . ." April breathed a sigh of relief. ". . . But then Rog arrived with his story. His point was that even though the two of you were just rigging Mr. Box, you *did* go out alone, which is against camp rules. And he said that since Todd is a senior camper who ought to know better, it was all his fault. To make a long story short, the *bad* news is that Rog is going to sing Todd's solo at the concert tomorrow night. I didn't have the heart to tell Todd."

"I can't believe him!" April fumed. "I hope he gets the world's biggest frog in his throat and can't sing a single note!"

"Me, too," Jackie agreed. "But look on the bright side. You haven't lost your solo."

"Yeah, I know," April said unenthusiastically. Somehow it didn't seem very important anymore.

Todd was waiting for her on the porch of the dining hall when she arrived a few minutes later. The lunch bell hadn't rung yet, so April suggested they take a walk. She felt it was her duty to tell him the bad news, and she didn't want to do it with everybody listening.

To April's surprise, Todd didn't seem the least bit upset. He just shrugged. "Hey, those are the breaks," he said, grinning. "There's always next year. I'm just glad that you're off the hook. Rog was right about one thing—it *was* my fault that you got into trouble, so if anyone deserves to lose a solo, it's me."

April shook her head vigorously. "It's not fair! You didn't force me to go with you. I went because . . ." She felt herself blushing.

"Because?" Todd repeated softly. He moved a little closer to her, and April shivered in spite of the warmth of the day.

"Just because," she mumbled, avoiding his intense gaze.

"I was hoping maybe you went because you liked being with me as much as I like being with you," Todd said. "And if you did, I was going to ask if you'd like to wear this." He fished in the pocket of his shorts and took out his name tag.

April caught her breath. "You—you were? I mean, you are? I mean . . ."

Todd smiled. "Yes, I was, and yes, I am, but only if we can trade. I know it's kind of late in the session since tomorrow's the last day of camp, but—well, I was kind of hoping we could see each other when we get back home."

"But what about Nancy?" April blurted out.

"Nancy?" Todd stared at her. "How did you know about her?"

April looked away. "Well, when I was looking through the mail I saw this pink envelope addressed to you," she confessed. "Actually, I think I smelled it before I saw it."

Todd threw back his head and laughed. "She did get a little heavy-handed with the perfume! That was her idea of a joke, I guess. Nancy's my cousin. We're real close, kind of like brother and sister, and she promised to write to me while I was at camp. I'm not very big on writing letters, so I call her every now and then to keep her posted."

"Your *cousin*? The girl you call is your *cousin*?" April cried, unable to believe her ears.

Todd nodded. "Yep. I called her the night the perfumed letter arrived, to tell her all about this terrific girl—you, April." He grinned. "I think she was kind of upset that I'd found somebody without her help! Nancy can be pretty bossy sometimes."

"You won't believe it," April said, "but all this time, I thought you had a girlfriend named Nancy back home!"

"No way," Todd said, putting his arm around her. "The only girl I care about is right here. Now will you trade name tags with me?"

April was so happy that she thought she'd explode. Throwing her arms around his neck, she whispered, "Oh, yes! I'll give you mine after lunch—it's in my cabin."

Just then the lunch bell began to clang. As soon as Todd had pinned his tag to the collar of April's shirt, they walked hand in hand back to the dining hall. It didn't take long for everyone to notice that they were now officially a couple, and April was thrilled that she belonged to Todd and he belonged to her, and not to some unknown girl back home.

April and Todd didn't see much of each other for the rest of the day. There were rehearsals all afternoon and evening for the final concert the following evening—full choir, Boys' Chorus and Girls' Chorus. Sunday morning and afternoon were filled with more rehearsals. April's solo went quite well, she thought, but so far she had only sung in front of the other campers and counselors. She just hoped she wouldn't freeze that night when her parents and hundreds of strangers would be in the audience.

When the last rehearsal was over late Sunday afternoon, April lingered, looking out over the Choir Bowl after the others had left. It hardly seemed possible that this was the last day of camp. Remembering how lonely and miserable she had been when she had first arrived, April smiled, starting to walk toward the dining hall. So much had happened in such a short time! In spite of Connie's jealousy and Roger's nastiness, she had had lots of fun. She'd mastered a lot of beautiful, difficult music, made new friends, and best of all, she had fallen in love with a boy who loved her, too, and who wanted her to be his girl.

Lost in thought, April didn't hear footsteps behind her on the path. A hand on her shoulder made her jump and she whirled around, to see her parents smiling at her.

"Hi, honey. Remember us?" her father teased.

"Dad! Mom! I didn't expect you so soon!" April cried, hugging them both. "I'm so glad you're here!"

As the three of them continued walking, April chattered happily, telling her parents everything she hadn't had time to put in her brief letters. At last Mrs. Sullivan said, "It sounds like you've had a wonderful summer."

April nodded. "I just love it here. The time went so fast! You were right, Mom. After I made some friends, everything was terrific. I can't wait for you both to meet my friends— one guy in particular." She felt herself blushing, and her parents exchanged amused glances.

When they reached the dining hall, April saw Karen standing with her mother and father in a long line of campers and their families who were waiting for supper. Karen waved and ran over to April.

"Mom, Dad, this is my friend Karen Sanchez," April said. "Karen's from Spring Valley, too."

As Karen shook hands with Mr. and Mrs. Sullivan, she said, "It's been so great getting to know April! Wait till you hear her solo tonight at the concert. And can you believe this?" She pointed to Todd's name tag, which April had pinned to the pocket of her shirt. When the Sullivans both looked puzzled, Karen giggled. "You mean you haven't told them yet?" she asked April.

"No, not yet." Then April looked closely at the name tag Karen was wearing and let out a little squeal. "You're wearing Jon's!"

Karen grinned. "And he's wearing mine. Isn't that neat? Well, the line's moving now, and I have to catch up with my folks. See ya later!"

"What's all this about name tags?" Mrs. Sullivan asked, peering at the tag on April's pocket. "And who's Todd Barrett?"

"He's the guy I want you to meet. It's a camp tradition to trade name tags when you find someone special," April said, beaming.

"Where is this special someone?" Mr. Sullivan asked.

"He's helping with the parking, but you'll meet him very soon."

Todd arrived just as April and her parents were finishing their meal. Glowing with pride, she introduced them.

"Our daughter seems to be confused as to who she really is," Mr. Sullivan joked, indicating Todd's name tag on April's shirt.

Todd grinned and pointed to the tag he was wearing. "Me, too." Then he turned to April. "Hey, guess what? I've got my solo back!"

"Oh, Todd, that's great. But how come? What about Roger?" April exclaimed.

"It seems he's in the infirmary with a bad case of poison oak," Todd said solemnly.

April laughed. *"Poison oak!* Oh, that's really too bad!"

"April, I'm surprised at you," her mother said. "The poor boy must be miserable."

Todd and April exchanged glances, trying not to laugh. "How did the 'poor boy' get it?" April asked.

"Probably from poking around in the woods the other night," Todd told her, his eyes dancing with amusement. "Well, guess I'd better grab something to eat before I change for the concert. See you later, April. Nice meeting you, Mr. and Mrs. Sullivan."

As soon as he had left, April showed her parents the way to the Choir Bowl and found seats for them in the second row, then dashed off to change.

It was total chaos in Cabin One, since all the other girls were dressing for the concert, too, but April managed to unzip her garment bag and take out the pale blue dress she had decided to wear. It was sleeveless with a full, swirly skirt, and when April put it on, her friends told her it looked great—she couldn't see it herself because everybody else was hogging the mirror. She was able to snatch only a quick glimpse of herself, just long enough to put on a little makeup and fix her hair, and then it was time to head back to the Choir Bowl with the others. The final concert was about to begin.

An hour later, the full choir had just finished Bach's "Mass in B Minor." April was proud that she had mastered not only the notes, but also the difficult Latin words. She could see her parents applauding vigorously and beaming at her.

Sandy nudged her. "Todd's next," she whispered.

As Paul Browning gave the downbeat, the Boys' Chorus began to sing their number. When it was time for Todd's solo, April thought he sang beautifully, even though it was only two bars.

Then the boys stepped back, and the Girls' Chorus, led by Mrs. Harper, launched into their Hungarian folk song medley. Connie's voice soared effortlessly on her solo, and

131

April had to admit that in spite of everything, Connie was really good.

As the enthusiastic applause died away, April felt her hands getting clammy. In just a few minutes, it would be time for her solo. What if she got stage fright the way she used to? Connie would love it if she froze, April knew, and that thought gave her the courage she needed.

The accompanist began the introduction to "The Rose." *This is it,* April thought as she stepped forward. The Girls' Chorus sang the first verse; now it was April's turn. She took a deep breath and started her solo. Was that really her own voice? As she sang, the words took on new meaning and April was swept away by the emotion of the song. When the last note faded away in the still mountain air, she knew she had never sung better. Mrs. Harper smiled and motioned for April to take a bow. The applause she received confirmed her success. In the second row, April's father and mother were clapping harder than anyone else.

I did it! she thought. *I actually did it!*

At intermission, Todd hurried over and hugged her. "You were terrific!"

April grinned at him. "So were you!"

"All two bars?" he joked.

"They were the best two bars in the song," April told him. "No one could have sung them better—certainly not Roger!"

"And you're not the least bit prejudiced in my favor?"

April beamed. "Not one bit!"

"Well, I have to see about my next song," Todd said.

"What next song?" April asked, surprised.

"Just wait—you'll find out," he said, and hurried offstage as the lights blinked off and on, signaling the end of intermission. It was time for the second half of the program, and most of the campers, including April, found empty seats in the auditorium.

Greg stepped out onto center stage where a spotlight shone brightly. He took a deep bow, and announced, "Ladies and gentlemen, welcome to Bear Mountain's Cabaret! We are proud to present some of the finest acts on this side of the Rockies. To start our show, here are the Riverside Madrigal Singers!"

One after another, the acts seemed to fly by, and April began to wonder if Todd had just been kidding when he had mentioned his next song. Then a poke in the ribs from Karen directed April's attention to the left side of the stage where Todd was stand-ing.

Greg came center stage again. "And now, for our next number, we proudly present Todd Barrett, with a new song he wrote here at camp."

"Maybe that's what he's been doing all week!" April whispered to Karen.

Todd strolled to the piano, flipped back imaginary tails and sat down. An exaggerated pantomime of flexing his fingers followed a toothy grin for the audience. Then he became serious as he played a soft introduction and began to sing in his rich tenor voice:

"Walking hand in hand with you
Is the thing I want to do.
Holding hands, exchanging words
We're walking hand in hand . . ."

April caught her breath as she listened to the lyrics. That was exactly the way she felt about him!

"It's for you," Karen whispered, her eyes dancing with excitement.

"Standing side by side with you
Is the thing I want to do.
Side by side in love with you
We're standing side by side . . ."

Todd looked up, searching the audience until he found April in the front row. He smiled at her, and April knew then that he *had* written it for her. It was as if everyone else had disappeared and she was alone hearing the special words:

"I have searched for someone true—
Now I've found that someone's you.
This song's for you to understand
That I want to walk beside you—
    Hand in hand."

A tear trickled down April's cheek. She felt suspended in time, caring only for the boy at the piano. When Todd finished singing, he smiled at her again. Then he got up from the piano, and the Choir Bowl exploded into cheers and applause. Todd took a bow and hurried offstage, heading straight for April. As the next act began, he slid into the empty seat beside her.

"Hey! What's this?" Todd reached up to wipe away the tear from her cheek. "I thought you'd like it."

"It was—*beautiful*," she cried, hugging him.

"Let's get away for a few minutes." Todd took her hand, and they slipped out of the Choir Bowl through a side entrance. They stood together, not speaking, looking up at the starry sky.

"It was a very special song, Todd," April murmured.

He took April in his arms. "I hoped you'd think so," he whispered. April could hear his heart beating as she leaned against his chest. Inside, tiny shivers raced through her. This was her dream come true!

Todd tipped her chin up and kissed the tip of her nose. April just smiled. She looked up into his eyes, and Todd bent down, brushing her cheeks and then her lips with soft kisses. This was no dream—this was real!

April melted into Todd's arms once more, and his lips pressed hers again, not gently this time but urgent and full of feeling. A thousand fireworks exploded within her.

"We'd better go back, Todd," she whispered when they finally drew apart.

"I know," he sighed. Sliding his arm around her waist, he walked with her back to the Choir Bowl. April's head spun and she felt that without his support, she'd collapse right there.

"I'm so sad that camp is over," she whispered.

Todd brushed a gentle kiss on her forehead. "But it's just the beginning for us. We'll be seeing a lot of each other from now on."

April smiled. This would always be the most important night of her life. She'd never forget this moment—with Todd, the music, and especially the magic of Bear Mountain.

Sweet Dreams

SWEET DREAMS are fresh, fun and exciting —alive with the flavor of the contemporary teen scene—the joy and doubt of first love. If you've missed any SWEET DREAMS titles, then you're missing out on your kind of stories, written about people like you!